MARQUESS OF FORTUNE

LORDS OF SCANDAL

BOOK 22

TAMMY ANDRESEN

LORDS OF TEMPTATION

Marquess of Fortune marks the end of the Lords of Scandal series. For any reader that has read along with me for the entire series, I love you. In all seriousness, I know you have a lot of choices and the fact that you've chosen me makes me feel humble and blessed.

If you are picking up Marquess of Fortune and haven't read any of the others, don't worry! Each of these is a stand alone and can be read all by its lonesome.

But either way, you're going to meet the Smith family and even though this is the end of the Lords of Scandal, it's not the end end. Coming in 2023 is the all new series, the Lords of Temptation. A spin off series, you'll meet a whole new cast and see some of your favorites from past Lords of Scandal books!

And thank you again for reading.

All my love,
    Tammy

MARQUESS OF FORTUNE

A spy, a liar, and a fraud, he's no woman's dream hero…

Lord Smith, known to his friends as Ace, has so many secrets, it's only a matter of time before his house of cards comes crashing down. His one goal is to secure his family's future by financing their gaming hell, Hell's Corner, before he's exposed. Which is why he can't afford to feel anything for the lovely Miss Emily Boxby. Especially not when he's trying to convince her brother to become his partner. But when trouble comes to call at Emily's door, thanks in part to his past, Ace throws his reservations to the side. He might not have a future of his own, but he'll see that Emily does, no matter the cost to himself.

One look into the dark depths of Lord Smith's eyes, and Emily is smitten. Perhaps that's why she trusts him even though she knows his past. Or maybe it's because she's always seen the good at his very core, carefully hidden behind his dark facade. But is that knowledge enough to overcome the forces at work around them?

Can they build a future from the ashes of his past?

This is a bridge novella that both completes this round of the "Lords of Scandal" series and introduces the spinoff series the "Lords of Temptation!" I hope you enjoy these rough-around-the-edges lords! The first book, *A Bet with a Baron*, will release in January 2023...

CHAPTER ONE

SOME MEN CONSIDERED THEMSELVES HONORABLE, brave, perhaps even kind... Ace was none of those men.

He was a spy.

The label wasn't entirely accurate. Far worse than just a spy, he could add imposter to his list of transgressions. Criminally so.

Liar. Most definitely. He could hardly keep track of them all.

Bastard. His father, the Earl of Easton, had sired Ace with his mistress.

Murderer, a definite possibility. He'd fired too many shots to count.

Was there a crime he hadn't committed? He rubbed the dark stubble on his chin as he considered.

He hadn't stolen from the crown.

And piracy...he'd not pillaged any boats at sea. That meant he wasn't entirely bad, was he?

The crimes he had committed, he'd done them all to protect his family. That had to count for something didn't it?

But needless to say, he didn't count himself among the good men. The ones who woke up and made the right choices, and deserved shiny futures and happily-ever-afters. Not that he believed anyone got that. But some people were content enough with their lives.

The most Ace could hope for was that he'd be able to secure his siblings' futures, all six of them, before he died or rotted in prison.

Caring for his siblings would be enough to consider his existence worth living. He didn't need marriage and who wanted to populate the world with more children anyhow? He had enough people to provide for as it was. He'd take care of them all somehow…

But the task proved rather difficult.

He sighed as a rush of dancers swirled by, their merry laughter at odds with his current mood.

It was a ball. Clearly, he was the one who was out of step. Literally. Standing against the wall brooding was not in keeping with the general air of merriment.

But he'd only come because his brothers had asked him too. As the oldest of the Smith brood, and the one who'd falsified family documents to make himself a lord of the realm, a hanging offense if he was caught, he'd come here on behalf of his family. His task, to convince a duke and a baron to become partners in his family's gaming hell, Hell's Corner.

He let out a growling noise of irritation, even thinking about that damnable club.

Hell's Corner had made his life infinitely more complicated. The damn place was supposed to have been a solution. Not another headache.

"How do you make that noise?" a soft voice asked to his right. High and feminine the sound skittered over his skin like a shiver.

When had he ever reacted like that to the sound of a woman's voice? It was odd and entirely unwanted. The last thing he needed in his life was another complication.

He pushed off the wall, determined not even to look at the woman whose voice had managed to cause such havoc. He turned and started moving away.

"Apologies," her breathy reply stopped his feet again. "I didn't mean to offend."

He let out a rumbling protest because he knew he'd been rude, and some decency deep within him demanded that he behave with a bit of social grace, even as his feet executed a sharp rotation back toward the female in question.

He didn't wish to see her.

He had no room in his life for any more problems and women, especially the type who would be at this party, rich and aristocratic, were always trouble.

But as he turned, he momentarily forgot his hesitation as his gaze met with wide, warm brown eyes fringed with dark lashes.

A pert little nose, full pink lips, and a pile of brown hair atop her head rounded out the vulnerable beauty that had stopped to speak with him.

"You did not offend," he answered, pulling his spine straighter and reminding himself that her company was unwelcome. "I simply don't wish for idle conversation. Hence why I was standing alone."

She cast her gaze down, her ridiculously long lashes casting over her cheeks that heated with a charming shade of pink. "Of course." She bobbed a quick curtsy, her delicate hands lifting out her skirts as she did. "I just thought…" But then she stopped. "Forgive me. Enjoy your evening."

And then she turned, her hair glimmering in the candlelight.

Which drew his eye to the slender column of her neck, the narrow set of her shoulders, and her tiny waist, highlighted by the band around her high-waisted gown. The pale pink silk caught the light as she began to retreat.

He'd never seen a woman who so immediately captured his attention. Both beautiful and vulnerable, he knew he should walk away as well. He'd started to…

"What's your name?" He'd spent enough time with the *ton* to know he shouldn't ask. A formal introduction was the only way to meet a woman like her. Though to be fair, she shouldn't have spoken to him either. Which led him to the question why she had spoken to him at all, and perhaps even more puzzling, why he called her back again. The request was beyond foolish.

She stopped and spun back to him, the blush still infusing her cheeks. "Miss Emily Cross."

"Miss Cross." He arched a brow, stepping closer. "Pleasure."

"And you, Lord Smith."

That made him pause. While he occasionally socialized, he rarely stepped out in society. He'd purchased the title for the express purpose of conducting business, not indulging in social events. "How do you know my name?"

She flushed even pinker, her chest rising and falling rapidly, which honestly had its merits. But he focused instead on the woman who knew him when she shouldn't. "I know your sister. Mirabelle."

Mirabelle? The elder of his two sisters, she was generally shy and quiet. And a bastard. Which meant, there was very little reason for any woman who would be attending the Spencers' Summer Soiree to know his sister. "How do you know my sister?"

She visibly swallowed, taking a half step back. "We volunteer together at the orphanage on Mondays."

He took a step forward and then another. Because that did not explain what she knew and did not know about his family and its wealth of secrets. His sisters didn't have friends outside each other and neither did his brothers. It was a rule they all adhered to in order to make the burden of such knowledge easier.

It had never been much trouble for him with so many brothers about, but he'd often wondered if it was harder for the girls. There were only two of them. Still, Mirabelle knew the rule and she'd clearly broken it. What had his dear sister shared with the lovely Miss Cross? Did the beautiful young lady know about his fake title and how he'd acquired it? Information like that would see him to the gallows. "Miss Cross, I'm afraid you're going to have to give me more information than that."

"I thought you didn't wish to converse?" she said, then slid back a bit further.

"No. I said I didn't care for idle conversation and this is anything but." And then he closed the distance between them, placing a firm hand under her elbow. With a deft turn, he started skirting the dancers as though he were taking her out to the courtyard.

But at the last moment, instead of stepping outside with several other partygoers who enjoyed the crisp fall air, he ducked them down a quiet hall, likely used by the servants.

Which meant they'd not be alone for long.

He'd have to use his time very wisely to discover what the pretty Miss Cross understood about his family's situation.

The secrets she might know could send him to the Tower, or worse, the gallows.

―――――

EMILY SWALLOWED down a lump as she stared up at the handsomely intimidating lord.

This was why she hardly spoke to anyone outside her family. Inevitably, the exact wrong words tumbled from her lips.

His dark eyes were narrowed as he stared back, his square jaw hard as granite. His hair was impeccably combed back from his face, his clothing equally perfect, which only added to his air of power and control.

She swallowed again. "My lord, we should not be here."

Somehow, his jaw further hardened. "What has my sister said to you?"

Oh. That.

A great deal actually.

Emily should have known to keep her mouth closed. She had a habit of saying the very thing that might upset a person most.

She didn't mean to, it just always came out that way.

And she'd heard so much about Lord Smith. Even seen him on a few occasions when he'd come to collect Mirabelle at the orphanage. Caught sight of his broad shoulders and strong stance through the window of the front room that the orphanage used for any visitors who might come calling.

He captured her attention every time she'd seen him from afar and she'd just...

She was in awe of him. She could barely manage the glittering world of the peerage and she'd grown up in it. How was he able to pretend to be something he had not been trained to be? And he did it so convincingly...

She knew he was a bastard.

Knew that his father, the earl, had helped him to procure documents from France to fake his lordship. They claimed he was the second son of a northern reclusive marquess. At least that's what Emily thought she remembered.

Knew that he used that false identity to provide for his four brothers and two sisters.

Knew that he held up the world around the Smith family without ever muttering a word of complaint or appearing to strain at all. At least according to Mirabelle.

That sort of strength stole Emily's breath and so when she'd seen him standing alone she'd just...

She'd wanted to meet him.

He stirred something in her that she was desperate to learn more about. Because, whatever those feelings were, they were the path to lead her to a real future. One where she might find a husband and cease to be an outcast.

She longed to leave behind the marriage mart where she was a failure and settle into a life as someone's wife. Caring for another, that was one place she hoped to be a success.

"You will tell me everything that Mirabelle has said about us, not leaving out a single detail."

She widened her eyes as she stared up at him. "Are you certain? That would take an excessive amount of time..."

He let out another rumble, remarkably like the first one she'd heard him make.

The sound conveyed strength, male will, and a certain disregard for others that fascinated Emily. She cared a great deal what others thought. Always.

She looked around. Any moment now, some servant or other would come down this hall and find them alone. "All right. If you insist." And she opened her mouth to begin.

But a noise down on the back stairs that surely led to the kitchen had them both looking up. With quick and decisive moves, his hand came to her elbow again as he guided her back out into the party.

She'd not wished to come.

To the soiree, that is. Her brother, the Baron of Boxby, had insisted that it would be good for her. As though her failures over the past two seasons would somehow be erased if she just tried again.

She'd had a few suitors. She was pretty enough. And as her brother was fond of saying, she had a good heart. But in these sorts of interactions, she tended to either be too quiet or say far too much. Exactly like now with Lord Smith. Or the men who'd been interested in her, hadn't really...suited.

Lord Smith's long, lean fingers on her elbow sent tingling sensations coursing through her. That was how a man should make a woman feel, wasn't it?

Not that he'd be interested in her. She didn't have that posh sophistication that handsome men enjoyed. And she shouldn't feel anything about him, not knowing what she knew about his past. His family. She didn't care that he was a bastard. It was a man's deeds that defined him, in her opinion, and this was a man who valued family and who used his strength to support them.

But as his fingers tightened, her heart did the strangest flop in her chest.

He started across the ballroom, guiding her along with him. "Where are we going?" she asked, trying to decide if she should be frightened or elated by this turn of events. It wasn't often she was swept away in such a tide of male...prowess.

"To find a more private place to speak," he muttered back.

"Oh no." She planted her feet, bringing them both to a stop. "I'm afraid I can't allow that."

"And I'm afraid that you don't have a choice."

But as she opened her mouth to explain that her brother had the power and the right to insist upon marriage should they be caught alone, her brother's voice rang out behind her.

"Emily?"

Her lips snapped shut as blood rushed in her ears.

Lord Smith looked down at her, his own mouth pressing into a firm line as his fingers tightened at her elbow. And then they were deftly turning toward her brother.

"My brother. Lord Boxby," she muttered to Lord Smith under her breath meeting her brother's gaze with a weak smile.

"Your brother is Baron Boxby?"

She didn't have time to confirm his question before her brother was upon them, two of his friends just behind.

The Duke of Upton and the Earl of Somersworth. Both men had placed dances on her card, but neither were the least bit interested in her. They'd asked her as a favor to her brother. Was that how her brother intended to turn around her fortunes this season? She hated being the object of their pity.

"Emily," her brother repeated, his gaze flitting to Lord Smith. "Where are you off to?"

Her mouth opened but no words came out. How did she even begin to explain?

Lord Smith, his hand slipping from her elbow, bowed. "A pleasure to make your acquaintance, Lord Boxby. I am Lord Smith."

Ken's eyes narrowed. "Smith?" he repeated, his shoulders straightening as he looked Lord Smith up and down. "How do you know my sister?"

"My sister volunteers alongside your sister at the orphanage."

Her brother visibly relaxed and Emily marveled at Lord Smith's ability to tell the truth and get away with it.

Well, that was *not* exactly right. One didn't get away with telling the truth. But he'd told the exact right amount of truth without revealing any of the unnecessary and unflattering details.

She glanced up at him, his face impassive and unreadable.

"How nice," Ken said, gaze assessing as he studied her. "Why haven't I met Lord Smith's sister if you're friends? You'll have to introduce us." Ken generally didn't approve of her friendships. She had a few friends but none that her brother liked. They were either shy like herself or not well-connected. Mirabelle was sure to be no exception.

"Since you're here." Lord Smith took a step toward her brother and away from her. "I've something that I'd like to discuss with you." Emily knew when she was being dismissed.

It was an experience she'd had often enough.

She wished she could grumble in dissatisfaction the way Lord Smith had. It was a lovely sound that commanded notice, and she didn't wish for her time with Smith to end. She'd been having fun. He'd dragged her to a private hall and then across the floor to another potentially illicit meeting. This might be the best ball she'd ever attended.

She'd like to marry someday. If she were being honest, she'd like to marry a man like Lord Smith. Strong. Commanding. How could she get a man like him to propose without some measure of experience?

Which was the only explanation for what she did next. "Lord Smith has asked me to dance."

All four men turned to her, her outburst clearly catching them by surprise.

Likely because they'd already forgotten her.

Lord Smith's eyes were wide as she slipped her hand into his elbow despite the fact that he hadn't offered it. "If you'll excuse us."

And then it was her turn to drag him across the floor.

CHAPTER TWO

The little chit.

Ace looked over at Miss Cross as she kept her eyes forward, tugging at his arm while she moved with as much determination as her delicate frame would allow. Was she avoiding his gaze?

She knew she'd interrupted. Then again, he'd been attempting to drag her off to question her so he supposed they were even in that regard.

How strange that she'd led him to the exact men he'd come here to meet.

He didn't know the earl…

But the duke and Baron Boxby were the exact two lords he'd come to offer partial ownership in his club.

Ace had spent the last several months working at another club, the Den of Sins.

Technically, that was the job that made him a spy. He'd told no one there that he owned a competing club and that his goal in spending the last of his money buying a stake in Den of Sins was to learn what made them better than all the other clubs and implement those practices into Hell's Corner.

It was an underhanded thing to do, and he hated himself for it, but his family had nearly run out of money and he had to find a way to make their business endeavor successful.

He tensed at the thought and Emily's fingers fanned out on his arm, giving him a light squeeze. Had she sensed his frustration? Was she comforting him?

He looked over at her again. It had been ages since someone had comforted him. What would it be like to actually rest his head in her lap or against her bosom, those arms wrapped about him?

He shook his head, banishing the thought. Hadn't he just got done saying he didn't need another person to care for at the moment? And wives led to babies, which created a whole lot more work. More responsibilities. More money.

They stopped in an open spot on the dance floor and Ace took Emily's palm in his, his other hand at her tiny waist.

Then again, for all she would need, she'd certainly give in return. He could feel that already. It was in her touch. Her eyes.

The music began and he started to move, her steps matching his with effortless grace. For a while they were silent and then finally, he leaned down close to her hear. "You've put me in a difficult situation."

"How's that?" she asked, leaning back so their gazes met again.

He tensed again at the warmth in her brown eyes. What was it about a woman with her back arched that was so damned appealing? He tightened his hand around the dip of her waist. "I was about to ask your brother to be a business partner with my brothers, which would mean revealing the truth about my family. But now you've insinuated that I've asked you to dance, which means your brother now considers me a potential suitor."

She gasped. "Oh, but it's one dance. Surely he doesn't think…" she trailed off, that pretty flush filling her cheeks again.

"A bastard like me shouldn't pursue a lady like you. Especially when he's about to ask her brother to be his partner."

Her chin tilted up then. "Then perhaps you shouldn't have been attempting to drag me off."

That was a fair point. "Perhaps you should not have accosted me when I was against the wall revealing you knew my family's secrets."

She caught her bottom lip between her teeth. "You're right. I shouldn't have."

Her admission caught him off guard. Usually, he had to fight for everything. To just have her admit she was wrong... He let out a sigh, realizing that he didn't wish to take the conversation any further. He'd said his piece and what was done was done. What was more, dancing with her was...nice.

Better, it was divine.

She moved with him effortlessly, her body fitting into his hand in the most perfect way. And those eyes gazing up at him...

He pulled her a touch closer. "Thank you for saying that."

And then she licked her lips.

Everything in him clenched.

"I'll make it right with my brother," she said, her gaze pleading with him.

He blinked in surprise. What did that even mean?

"Make it right?"

"I'll tell him the truth. I tricked you into dancing with me because I was curious. He's used to me doing foolish things that go awry. He'll forgive me. He always does."

He stared down at her, realizing that she intended to make herself look like the jester in order to further his agenda.

His fingers spread wide on her back, wishing that he could pull her against his chest. "You shouldn't—"

"It's all right. I don't mind."

He grimaced down at her, not sure what to say. They continued their dance in silence as they twirled about the floor along with the other dancers.

Had he been out of step before? Ace was in step now. What was more, he'd ceased thinking about his problems and for this moment, this dance, he just felt.

Leaning down closer, he caught a whiff of Emily's scent, softly fragrant and fresh as spring air after a rain, even the smell of her filled him with hope and a certain lightness.

And though he appreciated her offer to fall on the proverbial sword, Lord knew that he didn't get those offers often.

The idea didn't sit right.

Maybe it was her comment that her brother was used to her being the fool, what had she meant by that? And did the idea hurt her?

She was the sort of woman who should be protected, not ridiculed. He smiled to himself realizing that this was how he always ended up helping others rather than being helped. When it came right down to it, he was best suited to the role.

And that was why Ace would not allow Emily to tell her brother that she'd tricked him into the dance.

Instead, he'd tell the baron the rest of the truth. He was a bastard with a business proposition.

––––––––

EMILY SENSED some sort of shift in Lord Smith.

He'd gone quiet and he'd stopped demanding a recounting of all her conversations with Mirabelle. That was the first change. But there was something different in the way he held her too.

His grip was nearly possessive. She was close, almost indecently so, and his palm was pressed flat against her back, his fingers wide.

The touch had her heart hammering in her chest.

Even his fingers and palm conveyed strength. He moved her across the floor with masterful grace that stole her breath and the thoughts from her mind.

All she could do was feel. And every feeling filled her with delight and a deeper yearning that she hardly understood.

But if she might put it to words, she'd call it...wanting.

She wished for more of him.

The dance ended and his hand slipped from her back, the loss of that contact filling her with disappointment even as she placed her hand into the crook of his elbow.

Now that he'd touched her like that, she understood that she'd always wished for a man to do so. Would he ever again? The idea made her pulse with that wanting once again.

Would another man? But she could hardly think of anyone else as she snuck another glance at his profile.

He led her away from the floor and toward a dark corner of the ballroom. For a moment her heart sped up. Was he once again searching for a quiet place for them to speak? An image of him leaning close, his body all around hers, tempting, protecting, rose in her mind.

She'd give so much to experience that sort of embrace with him again. Her pulse thrummed in her ears at the very idea and tightened her grip on his arm.

But Lord Smith was not leading her to an illicit rendezvous in a quiet corner of the ballroom. Instead, he was leading her back to her brother.

Her brother stood with both his friends, a few matrons, and several debutantes. Emily ducked her chin and smiled, momentarily forgetting the riot of emotions coursing through her body, as she realized that a few marriage-minded mothers had caught her brother in conversation, and it would be some time before he was able to extricate himself from their grips.

And then her smile widened. This was her chance.

"We've a moment," she said, glancing up at Lord Smith. "Or two."

"Do we?" Lord Smith stopped walking and cocked a brow as he glanced down at her. Why did meeting his gaze almost hurt? He was near painful to look at.

She'd do nearly anything to extend this meeting. Even discuss the very topic she'd wish to avoid. What Mirabelle had told her about Lord Smith's family. "Did you have anything you still wished to ask me?"

Lord Smith glanced quickly at her brother and then back at her. "You're right. We do." He stepped in front of her, blocking her brother from view as he leaned closer. "What else has Mirabelle told you besides revealing our parentage?"

Emily swallowed, drawing in a quick breath. She'd started this conversation and so she'd finish it. Would her next words draw him closer to her or push him away? The latter thought made her chest tighten in painfully in her chest.

She'd wished to meet him for so long. Even from afar, he'd stirred something inside her that she wished to explore. Understand.

She'd made the choice to share with him to keep him by her side for a bit longer. She'd so little experience with such things, she hoped she hadn't just made a grave mistake.

CHAPTER THREE

HE STARED down at the delicate beauty, glad for the excuse to spend a few more minutes in her company and curious as to why she'd volunteered to share with him after all. What did she hope to gain by telling him what Mirabelle had told her?

"Just that you started a business to support the family but that it isn't going well."

A wave of irritation coursed through him. Just? That was a great deal. "She shared that, did she?"

Emily bit at her lip again and his thumb itched to smooth the worried flesh. "Don't be angry with her. It's a burden that she struggles with, I think."

He shook his head. Somehow, despite the roughness of the brothers in the family, or perhaps because of it, both of his sisters were sensitive. "I am not angry with Mirabelle."

Emily smiled at him then, a smile that lit her entire face and stole the reason from his thoughts. "Good. Because she loves you dearly."

He shifted, realizing that Mirabelle had shared far more with Emily than he'd even imagined. And he understood why. Emily was so easy to trust. "What else did she say?"

She hesitated, her lips pressing together and his own body tightened with impending dread. "That you met your half-brother, the new earl, and that isn't going well either."

Christ. Ace raked a hand through his hair. Mirabelle had told Emily about Ash? Was there a secret that Emily didn't already know?

He'd never met his father's only legitimate child, his half-brother, until a few months ago when he'd started at the Den of Sins.

Those lords all masked their identity with fake names so he'd had no idea that his half-brother worked there until he himself was too far embroiled in the deception to back out.

And also, if he were being honest, he might have been able to leave the Den of Sins. But he'd gone for good reason, to help his family and his business, and he could confess, he'd been curious.

They shared blood with the new Earl of Easton.

And family was everything to Ace.

"Is there anything Mirabelle didn't tell you?" he scoffed.

He'd have to chat with his sister tomorrow. Not that he'd give her too much trouble. He never could. Not where either of his sisters were concerned. But still. She'd broken a direct rule by bringing Emily into her confidence and she'd put him in even more danger. The more people in whom they confided...

Emily shrugged. "Anything she didn't tell me? I wouldn't know, would I?" She licked her lips stepping a bit closer as her eyes pleaded. "I promise your secrets are safe with me. Mirabelle and I understand each other, and I'd do anything to protect her. She's my friend."

"You understand each other?"

Emily's chin dropped then. "We're both on the outside looking in, I suppose."

Ace stared at her, perplexed. "Why are you on the outside? You firmly belong in this world." He said the words as much as a reminder to himself as he did to her.

She pressed her hands to the flat of the stomach. "I have a tendency to say too much or too little. Or exactly the wrong thing. I babble when I'm nervous and then I say way more than I should—like how I revealed I knew your sister or like...right now."

She stopped again, clamping her lips shut.

He could feel her hurt and embarrassment like a palpable force and he had the distinct urge to comfort her. But he fundamentally didn't understand the problem. Did men really care about social propriety?

He supposed there were times when it was inconvenient for a person to say too much. But the woman before him was lovely and warm and— He stopped. He'd found himself wishing for a future he'd never wanted before. One with a wife.

A sweet little brown-haired wife who snuggled close to him all winter long and whispered words of encouragement in his ear.

That was exactly the sort she was. He just knew she was tender and kind as surely as he knew that future would never be his. Inwardly he winced even as he straightened up and away from her. This sort of proximity was not to either of their benefits.

"I shouldn't have said all that, should I?" She fisted her hands, her teeth catching her lip again. "Now you're realizing everything I said was true, and you wish that you'd never asked, and—"

"Emily," he said, testing her given name on his tongue and finding that he liked it a great deal. "I wasn't thinking any of those things."

"Oh." Surprise rounded her mouth as she tilted her chin to look in his eyes.

He reached out and skimmed his fingers down the bare flesh of her arm between her sleeve and her glove, wishing his hand was bare so that he might feel her skin. He'd guess that it was achingly soft.

"But you are a proper lady and I am not at all a proper lord and—" He'd expected her to look relieved. He was giving her a very good explanation of why he'd been quiet but she didn't seem to enjoy his reassurances at all. In fact her features tightened, pain crinkling the corner of her eyes. "What are you thinking?"

"You don't have to give me excuses. I know who I am and what men think of me."

There it was again. Another assertion that she was inferior or unwanted.

"You've no idea what *I* think of you."

18

Her eyes widened at that, those lush lips parting as she looked up at him.

"Foremost, I think you're beautiful."

Her mouth dropped open even wider, her body going very still.

He should stop. None of what he was about to say would help him. In fact, it would make the next steps with her brother far more difficult, but he couldn't seem to make himself be quiet. That fact should have concerned him, control was his most reliable trait and he had too little in her company. In a matter of minutes, she'd worked past so many of his usual defenses. "I think you're warm and sweet, and your back has the loveliest curve I've ever touched."

Just when he thought her eyes couldn't go any wider, she blinked them rapidly, suddenly looking away. "Do go on."

He smiled at that. Just a small smile as he looked down at her. As much as he enjoyed saying the words, he realized she desperately needed to hear them, and he wished to make her happy. "I think I'd like to kiss you."

Her breath caught and held, and for a moment he worried she might not breathe until she let it out all in a rush. "That is…"

"But I also think your brother would sooner hang me than allow me to court you. As I already have an entire family to care for, and as I'm not doing a particularly good job of it, I'd be foolish to start anything new."

"Oh," she said again, lower and flatter, her regret evident in the single word. Did she want him too? Damn, but that made the aching need to touch her back again even more difficult to resist.

But as the two matrons who'd caught the baron in conversation shuffled off, Ace realized this was his chance. Much as he'd like to talk with Emily all night, he had a mission to complete. And if there was one trait he liked about himself it was that he'd do nearly anything for his family.

CHAPTER FOUR

EMILY WATCHED her brother disappear with Lord Smith and the Duke of Upton, disappointment like a physical ache forming in her chest.

She appreciated his compliments so much, and his honesty, but...

She felt as though she'd waited forever to meet a man like Lord Smith. He held some key that unlocked her future, she was sure of it. But how she could she decide exactly what part he played if she couldn't spend time with him?

But she felt as though she'd just gotten a taste of what could be and now he was slipping through her fingers.

"It's our dance, my lady," the Earl of Somersworth said from her right.

Drat. She'd nearly forgotten he was there.

She looked over at him, his dark blond hair and chiseled jaw making him rakishly handsome. Loads of ladies must fancy him.

But she didn't feel anything but minor annoyance at the interruption. "It's quite all right, my lord. You needn't dance with me."

"Not dance?" His brows drew together. "I am here for the sole purpose of dancing with you." And then he gave her a deep bow.

That should have been flattering. She gave him the best smile she could, though she suspected it was weak. Because it wasn't her he'd come for but her brother. "The next time Lord Boxby tries to make you lay favor on me, I give you my full consent to tell him to bugger off."

Somersworth quirked a single brow and then his gaze swept down her as though he were seeing her for the first time. "You don't wish for my attention, Emily?"

He'd never used her given name like that before. No man had, but now it had happened twice in a single evening. "Your attention is most welcome, my lord."

She didn't really mean that, but it was the polite thing to say. Normally, she'd be tempted to utter something foolishly close to the truth, but with sudden realization she understood why it was better not to tell him she didn't have those sorts of feelings for him.

He didn't really feel them for her either. He was just smarting a bit from her rejection. "But your attention because you wish to give it and my brother's insistence that you do are very different. I'll capture a man's attention or I won't, but I'll not trick him into thinking I'm more desirable than I actually am. That doesn't feel…right."

Somersworth gave her a nice smile, admiration shining in his eyes. "Something has shifted in you, dear Emily, and I have a feeling that your fortunes are about to change with or without our dance." Then he stepped even closer, holding out his hand. "But all the same, I'd like to dance with you now. Not because Boxby asked me, but because you shine brightly tonight and every man here will want you on his arm." Then he leaned even closer with a wink. "Especially me."

A flush of appreciation filled her cheeks. While she knew Somersworth flattered her, she appreciated the words. He was more like a brother to her than anything else, but she couldn't deny that his praise made her shoulders a bit straighter.

And she could clearly see that others had taken notice.

Several men watched her and Somersworth's progress to the dance floor. She felt their eyes, an intensity to their stares she'd never known before.

Somersworth stopped in an open spot taking her in his arms as the music began to swell.

His wheat-colored eyes intent upon her as he started to move.

Emily could appreciate the masculine aura that surrounded him, the power he effortlessly wielded. But she could also sense the difference between this dance and the one she'd just had with Lord Smith.

She felt none of the breathless wonder that had gripped her in Lord Smith's arms.

"Tell me you're not actually interested in him." Upton's words once again pierced into her bubble of thoughts. Had he heard them?

"Interested in whom?" she asked, looking over the crowd of dancers so as to avoid his piercing gaze.

"I know you're thinking of Smith."

She caught her lip, still not meeting his eyes. "I was not."

"Yes, you were. You had this dreamy look on your face," he said sounding a bit put out.

She finally looked at him, her own eyes shining with a question. "You don't know me well enough to read my face."

He shook his head. "Emily. You don't know me well enough to read mine. But I have noticed you even when you're not paying a bit of attention to me."

She drew in a sharp breath, blinking several times. How had she missed this? A surge of feminine pride coursed through her as she stared at the handsome earl. Could it be true? And how did that change all that she'd thought about herself and assumptions she'd made about her future? She'd considered her prospects dim at best. "My lord?"

He raised a brow. "If I'm going to be bested by another man, tell me it's not going to be him of all men."

"What do you mean?" she asked, trying not to allow him to read her face this time though she suspected her emotions were written all over her features. Somersworth knew she fancied Smith but what did he know about Lord Smith's past?

"He isn't what you think," Somersworth said pulling her a touch closer. "Don't allow him to fool you, Emily. You're much too...good... to be taken in by a man like that."

She frowned. Did Somersworth know Lord Smith's secret too?

Did she tell Somersworth that Lord Smith had already rejected her? "I doubt very much I am too good for him, my lord."

"You don't give yourself enough credit."

She looked at him, cocking her chin to the side to study him. The façade she'd been able to maintain slipped away again as she asked a question far more like her usual self. "And am I too good for you as well? Is that why you've never pursued me?"

He spun her about the floor, his grip at her waist firm. "It is." He didn't seem to be jesting. In fact, he sounded deadly serious, which honestly surprised her. When had she, Emily Boxby, managed to procure multiple men's interests? The idea was heady and wonderful. "Lord Somersworth?"

His grip tightened. "But know this, if it's between me and him, I'll be damned if I let him just steal you away. Whatever my flaws, they are a fair sight better than what he offers."

Emily gasped, so surprised that she nearly tripped on her own feet. Somersworth kept her moving with all the grace and prowess she'd expect from a man like him.

It was almost a pity he didn't make her heart trip over itself the way Lord Smith had. Lord Somersworth would be so much less complicated...

————

ACE SAT IN A PRIVATE STUDY, glancing about at the understated opulence that surrounded him. Rich mahogany wood lined the walls while plush velvet-covered furniture filled the room.

Nor was it lost on him that these rooms would normally be closed off to guests, but the baron and duke had been provided access to the family's private spaces with barely a whispered word.

These were the sort of resources he hoped to access by making these men his partners.

Of course, he might have asked his legitimate brother, but when Easton had discovered who Ace was...

They weren't speaking.

23

In fact, Ace wouldn't be surprised if the Earl of Easton challenged him to duel the next time he saw his bastard brother.

But he digressed.

And while his own death was a possibility, he needed to focus on what he might change before anything happened to him.

Clearing his throat, he settled into the chair across from the baron, accepting the offered cheroot.

"You wanted to see me, Lord Smith?" the baron asked, using a nearby candelabra to light his smoke.

"I did."

"You understand that I can't allow you to court my sister."

A muscle in Smith's jaw ticced as he took a moment to collect himself. He didn't wish to court Emily. But his stomach disagreed as it gave a lurch of disappointment. "That's not why I'm here."

"Good," Boxby said and then drew in a deep puff. "I know the truth about you, and while I have no desire to cause trouble, I also have no intention allowing you to marry my sister."

Well, at least his meeting wasn't entirely ruined, in fact, it might be even easier if the baron knew the truth about him. He was here for a purpose...his family. And in that regard he still had a chance at success. He ought to be happy.

But he liked Emily far more than he should after a single meeting.

"Understood," he answered, leaning forward in his chair. "Which leads me to my point—"

"Why were you dancing with her then?" the duke asked, his voice so deep, it rumbled out of his chest, filling the room.

Ace arched a brow, attempting to look unconcerned. "Miss Boxby is friends with my sister and I know a bit about her struggles..." He was making it sound as though he'd danced with her out of pity and he hated himself for it. She deserved so much better than that.

But the other two men visibly relaxed.

And the duke chuckled. "She is as sweet as she is kind, but she could use a bit of help."

Boxby grimaced. "Not that much. She's pretty too. Don't forget that. She just needs a bit of a push in the right direction is all. And she needs more confidence. If there is one thing she lacks, it's that."

Smith relaxed, hearing the other man's brotherly concern. He knew all about that. "I'm sure you're right." The baron gave him a long look and Ace knew it would be best to steer the conversation away from Emily all together. Clearing his throat, he started again. "The reason I came tonight, the only reason, was to speak with the two of you—"

"Us?" the Duke of Upton asked, his brows rising.

"You," he repeated. "I have a gaming hell…"

"The Den of Sins?" Upton said as he straightened. "I heard you were in league with those lords. Quite the reputation that place has."

Ace's teeth ground together. "Well, I am a partial owner in that venture, as well, but the club I'm here to discuss is Hell's Corner."

"Hell's Corner?" Boxby asked his brow furrowing. "Never heard of it."

Ace held in a growl of frustration. "And that's why I'm here. After taking part in the Den of Sins, I have a very good idea of how to turn Hell's Corner—"

"Into another Den of Sins?" Upton asked.

"Something like that." He knew he was glowering. But this entire conversation was a reminder of how his legitimate brother had the successful club and the successful life while he was close to drowning in money troubles. And his siblings would go down with him.

"What do you want from us?" Boxby asked, leaning forward as a ring of smoke wreathed his head.

"We're looking for partners."

"We?" Upton asked. "Who else has agreed to this venture?"

Ace ignored the question for the moment. "Men who can get in on the cheap and then make twice the fortune that the lords in the Den of Sins have made."

Thanks first to thieves and then his legitimate brother, Ace had hardly seen any of those assets but he knew they existed. What he didn't know was how hard he could press to actually receive his share from the Den of Sins. He'd paid in just like the other men, but it was another way in which he'd yet to win.

Another issue with being a fraud. It didn't give much sway to push for his actual rights.

Boxby gave him a calculating look as he drew the cheroot from his mouth, holding it between two fingers. "What kind of money did they make in the Den of Sins? Have you made? And what about Hell's Corner? Can you get us statements?"

Ace scrubbed his chin, his eyes briefly closed, knowing that it was unlikely he'd be able to get any paperwork from the Den of Sins. But then he snapped them open again. No point in giving up before he'd tried. He was nothing, if not persistent. "If I can, would you be interested?"

Upton pushed off the mantel. "I would."

Ace drew in a fortifying breath. At least he hadn't gotten a hard no. And now…he'd need to see his legitimate brother who hated his guts and convince Easton to give his bastard brother financial statements on the club for which he'd yet to pay Ace a single penny of the money owed.

Easy.

He thought about Emily in his arms during their dance. How he'd like to hold her again. She'd been a welcome reprieve from the rest of his life.

CHAPTER FIVE

THE FOLLOWING MONDAY, Emily stood just inside the orphanage's foyer next to the door, Mirabelle to her right, their arms linked. The sun shone in through the windows, speckling the floor with patches of merry light.

"Are you certain your carriage was supposed to pick you up at one?" Mirabelle asked as she craned her neck to peek out the nearby window.

"I'm certain," Emily lied to her friend as her chest tightened in guilt. She knew that her carriage was not due to arrive until nearly two.

She nipped her lip.

Perhaps she should have just told Mirabelle the truth. She'd created this ruse to see Mirabelle's brother, Ace.

Dastardly, she knew.

But the Earl of Somersworth's words had been echoing in her head for days. Had she mistaken her feelings for Smith?

Had she allowed her fancy for him before they'd even met to color her dance with him? Make her believe there was an excitement there that didn't actually exist?

And if it did, if what she'd felt was real, what of her decision to attract his attention? If she could learn to do that, then surely, she'd be ready to find a husband.

Much as Emily suspected that she had a special connection with Lord Smith, she wished... Well, she wanted to be married. And partly why she'd wished to meet Smith in the first place. Somehow she knew that what he stirred in her was the key to unlocking her feminine power, which she desperately needed to find.

She'd been invisible for so long. And one meeting with Lord Smith, Ace, and another man, an earl, had expressed his interest.

What was more, the earl was handsome, powerful, and even more unbelievable, he wanted her. Emily Boxby. Awkward sister to the baron. In so many ways she logically knew that Lord Somersworth was a sounder choice.

There were no questions about his title. He was already friends with her brother. A life with him would be so easy.

Her stomach churned at the idea of marrying a man she didn't love. Would she grow to feel the emotion in time? Somersworth had always been so kind.

Perhaps she'd misunderstood her reaction to Lord Smith.

Maybe she'd simply reacted to any handsome man laying favor on her and if she saw him again...

She'd realize what?

That Lord Smith wasn't special. That her reaction to him was just her aching heart responding to the attention of a handsome man. But she'd had these feelings before they'd even met and...

She drew in a shuddering breath. There was only one way to know for certain. And that was to see him again.

"I'm sure it's all right." Mirabelle patted her arm, mistaking Emily's source of emotional distress. "Likely your driver just became confused."

Her driver and footman were accustomed to her weekly trips to the orphanage and left her in the care of the headmistress of the facility, arriving to pick her up at promptly two in the afternoon every Monday.

"I'm sure you're right," she answered with a weak smile. She hoped

Mirabelle mistook that weak smile for worry and not guilt. "They'll be here soon."

"My brother will be here any moment." Mirabelle continued patting. "If your carriage hasn't arrived, we can escort you home."

Emily's heart jumped. That was the exact invitation she'd hoped for and yet more guilt twisted her stomach. "Oh, that's not necessary. I'm sure they'll be here at two. They likely just forgot the change in schedule." *Because I never told them.*

Mirabelle shook her head. "I insist. You'll like my brother. He's very noble when it comes to caring for others."

Emily winced as she turned to Mirabelle. She should have told Mirabelle earlier as they chatted while serving the orphans their noon meal. But it had been busy and she'd not known where to begin. "I...I met him."

"You did?" Mirabelle's eyes grew wide. "When?"

"The soiree on Saturday evening," She bit harder on her lip. "I recognized him and he spoke with my brother..." She was bungling her words. Not wanting to lie. Afraid to tell Mirabelle that she'd developed a bit of a crush...

Mirabelle's eyes grew wide. "Your brother is the baron my brothers have been discussing?"

Emily blinked in surprise. On that account she could truthfully plead ignorance. "I have no idea."

But Mirabelle's hand was tightening on her arm. "My family needs help, Emily. Do you think—" And then her friend stopped, her lips tugging into a frown. "I'm sorry. I shouldn't even ask."

"Ask what?" Emily covered Mirabelle's hand with her own. Mirabelle was about to forthright ask for the favor she needed, unlike what Emily had done this afternoon. "You know if there is any way I could help you, I would."

"Is it possible to plan an evening together? Something that might help my brother. He never asks for it, but I think he might need it."

Emily drew in a breath. After what she'd done today, it was the least she could do. "I'll do my very best."

Mirabelle released a long breath. "Thank you."

The sound of carriage wheels interrupted them both and they turned toward the door. Lord Smith had arrived.

In moments, he appeared in the doorway.

Emily's heart stopped in her chest, then stuttered to wildly beat again.

Whatever fiction she'd been attempting to convince herself existed, vanished. This was not about a random man who'd given her a crumb of attention. The sight of Lord Smith's handsome face, strong jaw, and piercing eyes stole her voice and her reason as she stared up at him, lips parted.

"Miss Boxby," he rumbled with a short bow. Then he turned to his sister. "Mirabelle."

"Ace," Mirabelle replied as she let go of Emily and stepped up to kiss her brother's cheek.

He dutifully bent down, his features visibly softening. The air rushed from Emily's lungs. She'd like to see him look at her like that.

"Did you have fun?"

Mirabelle wrinkled her nose. "We feed needy children. It's rewarding, not fun."

Lord Smith's brows lifted. "I see. Apologies for not understanding the gravity of your endeavor."

Mirabelle swatted at his arm playfully. "I heard you met my friend," Mirabelle said, turning toward Emily. "Isn't she wonderful?"

"Quite." But his face was a blank mask as he turned to look at Emily again.

"It's a pleasure to see you again as well, my lord," Emily answered as she swallowed down a lump. Those words didn't even begin to describe the well of emotion pulsing through her.

Drat it all.

"Emily's carriage is late." Mirabelle gave her brother's arm a squeeze. "Might we escort her home?"

Emily noted the frown that graced Lord Smith's lips before he covered the look with a blank stare. "I've an important meeting that I need—"

"Ace," Mirabelle chastised, her voice sharp. "I can't just leave her here."

"In the company of the headmistress?" Ace's brows shot up.

"Don't be a ninny," Mirabelle replied. "What if there had been an accident with her carriage? What if—"

"Forgive me," Lord Smith rumbled over his sister, stopping her words. "Of course, we can escort a lady in need. Shall we?"

Mirabelle let go of her brother's arm and stepped aside for Emily to take her position.

Her plan had worked.

But as she slipped her hand into his elbow, she was fairly certain she'd lost. Because while she knew her feelings from the soiree had been real, she'd learned something else.

He didn't appear to share them. But even as her chin dipped, she remembered the words he'd said before he'd left with her brother at the ball. The ones where he'd called her pretty and whispered that he'd wished to kiss her.

Perhaps, she could remind him of those feelings once again. If this was a journey of discovering more about herself, no one would teach her more than Lord Smith.

Which was why she needed to attract his attention once again.

———

THE FEEL of Emily's hand on his arm had Ace's pulse thrumming through his veins. That feeling of wanting to kiss her returned with a vengeance.

What had this woman done to him?

He'd been rude refusing the ride initially. But the idea of her in his carriage, it undid him in ways he couldn't articulate. They'd be close. The intimacy alone made his heart speed in his chest.

But also, that was his space. His father had purchased the vehicle years ago and had bequeathed the carriage to him on his twentieth birthday.

At the time, he'd been thrilled. But now the carriage seemed like a consolation prize compared with the riches that had been bestowed upon his legitimate brother.

His father had always maintained that Ace's mother had been his real wife and Ace and his siblings his real family.

How did that make Easton feel?

As a child, he'd assumed something was wrong with the countess and her son. They weren't lovable.

But now that he was older, he realized they'd all suffered because his father had chosen to divide his time, his money, and his affection over two families. It was beyond selfish and a mistake he'd never make.

It was also a reminder of why a committed relationship would never work for him. Especially with a woman like Emily. Romance between classes always led to heartbreak, no matter how well-intentioned.

That thought enabled him to hand Emily into the carriage and then calmly take the seat across from her.

He watched as she pressed her skirts into place, Mirabelle giving him a glowing smile as she did the same. "Your address, Miss Boxby?"

"Oh. Yes." She flushed, looking down at her lap and his gut tightened. He loved her blushes. "Seventeen Adams Row. It's near Grosvenor Square."

With a nod, he rapped on the wall behind him and called out the address to his driver. A driver he'd have to give up soon if this plan failed.

Emily drew in a deep breath, her chest swelling as she did. His gaze dropped to her bosom. Her breasts weren't exactly large, but compared with the rest of her...

He remembered his thought the other night about how he'd like to seek comfort on such a chest.

But at this moment, he'd like to do a bit more than that.

His body clenched and he snapped his teeth together to fight against the rising tide of attraction.

"Tell me about the soiree." Mirabelle turned to Emily. "Did you dance with a great many men?"

Emily's brown eyes flicked to his before they returned to her lap. "A few."

Ace rolled his head back and forth. "I had the pleasure of dancing with your friend."

Mirabelle gave him a sparkling smile. "Did you?"

Emily nodded. "He was very kind."

Kind?

But Mirabelle answered before he could argue. "Ace is a good dancer. He taught both myself and my sister."

Emily's surprised gaze rose to his again.

"My sister exaggerates. She had a tutor."

"Only until I was thirteen." Then Mirabelle leaned forward. "That's when our father passed."

Ace grimaced. He never shared this information and he hated doing it even now. Even with Emily. Those had been difficult days when they realized how much their lives would change now that their father was no longer their benefactor. Nearly all of the assets had gone to the legitimate heir. And the burden of caring for his mother and siblings had fallen to him.

"I'm sorry for your loss," Emily said without a bit of judgment in her voice. "We lost our parents at the same time and my brother had to take over my education as well. I think he blames himself for my failures."

Ace stared at the woman across from him. Not only did she not judge them for grieving a father they hadn't the right to miss, but she shared a bit about herself too.

"I highly doubt he thinks you the failure you think yourself," he said despite himself. He needed to comfort her.

Emily gave him an appreciative smile. "Thank you for that."

Mirabelle tapped her arm. "Who else did you dance with? What did they serve for food? How many candles light the ballroom?"

Emily looked at Mirabelle with a bit of a laugh. "I danced with the Earl of Somersworth and I honestly can't remember what they served. It's all the same. Mutton. Bread. Cheese. But hundreds of candles light the room. You have to be careful of the dripping wax. It has the potential to ruin your dress."

But Ace hardly heard most of what she'd said. He'd been under the impression that she rarely socialized with men at these parties. "You danced with the Earl of Somersworth?"

Even he could hear the sharp edge to his voice.

Emily's eyes widened as she cocked her head to the side, giving him a long stare. "Yes. I did."

Jealousy shot through him like a flash of lightning.

Which was ridiculous. He had no right for any such feelings and they'd only bring him misery. Of that he was certain. But his fist still clenched as he considered just how right for Emily a man like Somersworth would be.

CHAPTER SIX

EMILY TRIED to catch her breath as Lord Smith, Ace, glowered at her across the carriage.

If she didn't know any better, she'd think him jealous.

But Mirabelle didn't seem to notice the undercurrent running between Emily and her brother and she continued on. "Oh, did you? A real earl? Was it as dreamy as I imagine? Tell me everything!"

Everything? Emily's skin prickled from awareness as Ace watched her from his seat, his attention unwavering. Could she really tell Mirabelle, in front of Ace, about how Somersworth had confessed having feelings for her? Hinted at marriage?

Her cheeks flushed with heat at the very idea. Would it anger or him or would it possibly make him jealous? That notion had her shifting in her seat...

Across from her, Ace let out that growling rumble she found so arresting and she jumped in her seat.

"Yes, Miss Boxby. Tell us everything."

Her fingers trembled and she carefully folded them in her lap to hide the reaction. "There isn't much to tell. He's my brother's friend."

"Is he handsome?" Mirabelle asked letting out a dreamy sort of sigh.

"Yes," she answered honestly, having no idea what else to say. The right words always failed her when she was nervous.

Ace let out an even deeper noise of dissent. "Did he tell you how lovely you were?"

This conversation was surely not happening. She swallowed a lump as nerves of excitement and dread fluttered through her. "Why would he..." She simply couldn't lie again today. Deceiving wasn't something she did naturally and she already felt an immeasurable amount of guilt about her earlier fabrication to Mirabelle. And honestly, she couldn't knowingly cause Ace to be jealous. If that's what he was even feeling. It didn't feel right to make him hurt in anyway.

"Oh, he did, didn't he?" Mirabelle gushed, touching her chest as she fanned herself and then sat back with a sigh. "How romantic."

Emily kept her lips pressed together. Her gaze flitted up to Ace's to find him glowering back. "Tell us, Miss Boxby, did he confess his affection?"

Emily licked her suddenly parched lips as she shifted in her seat. This is what falsehoods brought her. She deserved this uncomfortable grilling. Had she hurt Ace's pride? His feelings? Just a tiny bit of hope shined through her guilt. "He didn't spout poetry or anything. Likely, he simply danced with me because my brother asked him to. Baron Boxby wants to help build my confidence. And Lord Somersworth just..."

But Ace's glower only grew darker. "He just noticed that you were as beautiful as you were effervescent."

Mirabelle gave a decided squeak at her brother's words.

Emily opened her mouth to reply but found no sound came out at all as pleasure at the compliment coursed through her.

Ace sat back in his seat, his brows drawn tightly together, his arms crossed. "If he offers, you should accept."

Those words knocked the breath out of her—and all her joy too.

If she'd been elated by his obvious jealousy, he robbed her of all the air with his last sentence. He'd told her he didn't wish to marry. And then there was his false life...

And she'd told herself that she'd only furthered her relationship with Lord Smith to discover more about herself.

But somehow, that dismissal gutted her. "Forgive me, my lord," she said, her voice trembling with emotion. "But I did not ask for your advice."

He straightened, his brows shooting up. "I beg your pardon?"

She lifted her chin as she held back stinging tears of hurt. "I don't need your advice on my future."

His mouth opened and then closed. "I see."

The carriage turned and she knew they were a minute or two from her home. She looked over at Mirabelle. "I'll speak to my brother about your request." She owed Mirabelle that after what she'd done today.

Mirabelle nodded but her eyes were now darting from Emily to Ace. "You don't have to—"

"Nothing would make me happier," she said, reaching for her friend's hand. "I'll send word to you."

Mirabelle nodded, giving Emily's fingers a squeeze. Then she leaned over and whispered in Emily's ear. "Meet me in Hyde Park tomorrow at two in the afternoon."

"All right," Emily replied as the carriage drew to a stop.

Ace snapped open the door and climbed out, holding out his hand to her. Reluctantly, she slipped her fingers into his, his strong grip sending a shiver of awareness through her.

She bit her lip to keep from visibly trembling.

If Ace were jealous of Lord Somersworth, he didn't intend to do a thing about it. In fact, he'd encouraged her to accept the other lord's suit.

Lifting her skirt with her free hand, she started down the steps, her other hand still encased in Ace's much larger fingers.

"Emily?" her brother asked.

Her chin snapped up, her brother, His Grace, and Lord Somersworth all stood on the top step. "Ken?"

A brick settled in the pit of her stomach.

"What are you doing home early and with him?" her brother

barked, trotting down the steps so quickly that she froze halfway down the vehicle's steps.

Drat. Everyone would soon know that she'd lied.

"Emily?" Mirabelle asked, poking her head out of the carriage. "Is everything all right?"

Her brother skid to a stop, several feet away, staring at Mirabelle. "Who is that?"

"Lady Mirabelle Smith, may I introduce you to my brother, Baron Boxby." Emily stepped down, Ace's fingers still firmly holding hers.

"A pleasure." Mirabelle gave a tentative nod.

Lord Somersworth stepped around her brother and came to her other side, taking Emily's other hand in his. "Come, Miss Boxby." His lip curled slightly as he looked at Ace. "We should get you out of the sun."

Ace's lips thinned across his teeth as he held her fingers just as firmly, not relinquishing them for the span of several seconds.

Emily held her breath before she finally came to her senses. And with a decided tug, she pulled her hand from Ace's. He was the one who'd told her to accept the Earl of Somersworth's suit. Not that there was one, but he didn't need to know that for now.

She'd arrange a meeting between her brother and Ace for Mirabelle's sake. And then she never wanted to see Ace again.

———

ACE BROUGHT his sister to their Cheapside home and then started back across town to see the Earl of Easton.

He should be preparing for this meeting with his half-brother.

It had been a shock that Easton had agreed at all. And the fact that he had told Ace that other man was planning something awful.

His brother was sure to try and either verbally or physically best Ace. But all Ace could think about was a brown-haired beauty who'd artfully maneuvered a meeting with him today. He knew very well her brother had not forgotten to send the carriage.

She'd wanted to see him.

And he'd rejected her.

It was for her own good, he reasoned. Marrying a bastard would bring her nothing but heartache.

The idea of her marrying the Earl of Somersworth had cut him into a thousand pieces.

He'd seen the possessive way the other man had taken her hand, glaring at Ace over the top of her head. He wanted Emily for himself and he'd likely get her.

His fist clenched in his lap as he repeated how he didn't wish to marry.

But the words rang hollow.

Because a wife so loving and sweet would surely soothe some of the ache that had settled into his shoulders. He wanted Emily. Hell. He might need her despite his best attempts to push her away.

But it wasn't fair to her.

Not when she had a much better option than him. Didn't she see that? Why had she sought out Ace today if she had the offer of an earl?

The carriage stopped again and he slowly lifted himself off the bench he'd slumped against, smoothing back his hair.

He should cancel. Reschedule.

He'd need every ounce of control to face his half-brother and he had almost none left. He could feel emotions he usually buried deep simmering just under the surface.

But if he didn't attend today, would his half-brother ever see him again?

Mirabelle needed him to do this and do it well.

Anna needed him to succeed.

Rush, Triston, Gris, and Fulton were all depending on him.

He snapped open the door and started down the steps, making his way to the Earl of Easton's front door.

It swung in before he'd even made it to the top of the wide granite steps, a starched and straight butler eyeing him from the doorway. "Lord Smith, I presume?"

Ace listened for any trace of disdain but caught none. "That's right."

"Right this way, my lord. His lordship is expecting you."

Ace followed the man up a wide set of stairs, polished and gleaming, up to a stately landing and down a wide hall to a study that overlooked a perfectly manicured garden.

Ace liked their home, it was comfortable, and large enough, and it had the advantage of being entirely theirs.

But this was elegance on another level.

Easton sat behind the desk, his gaze meeting Ace's, his look impassive and unreadable. "Ace."

"East."

The other man gestured for Ace to sit. "To what do I owe the pleasure of a visit from my nefarious brother?" East's voice held a hard edge that Ace ignored.

They shared the same jaw. Hard and lean. And their eyes were different colors but the shape... "Nefarious?"

"Did you or did you not infiltrate the Den of Sins to root out our secret to success? Or was it me personally on whom you were spying?" There was the derision Ace had been expecting. It was almost a relief. That he knew how to deal with.

They weren't wasting time, apparently. "The former. I had no idea you were, well, you."

East gave a quick nod. "I appreciate that bit of honesty."

Ace sucked in a breath. "I've never lied."

East scrunched his brow as he stared across the desk. "How do you figure that?"

"No one asked, 'Do you own another club?' They only asked if I was interested in funding the Den of Sins and working there one day a week."

East's eyes grew larger. "I suppose that's true."

"And I didn't learn anything I might not have gleaned as a patron. Make the interior plush. The liquor exotic and expensive, the dealers attractive." He drew in a breath. "Unless you count, keeping track of earnings to make certain you don't have thieves. I did learn that bit from being an owner."

East's jaw hardened. "So you yourself never stole from us?"

Ace's brows drew together. "Of course not. Why would you think that?" He straightened in his chair.

"Because…" East's mouth twitched. "At least one man we know of still eludes us."

"I thought you found the thieves and killed them?"

East tentatively shook his head. "We've not."

And then he reached down, lifting a satchel and setting it on the table with a heavy thump, the contents clinking inside.

"What's that?"

East ran a hand through his short, cropped hair. "It's your original buy-in plus the royalties owed to you."

The money was a welcome sight, but he knew what it meant. "I'm no longer a partner at the Den of Sins."

"You're not."

He didn't care exactly. He'd never meant to be a long-term partner. But this dismissal was tied in with his personal relationship with East. He'd been rejected in every way possible by his legitimate brother and that hurt him deeply. "You are my blood. I'd never steal from you."

East showed his teeth. "You've taken from me my entire life."

Ace glared across the desk, his hand slapping down onto the arm of his chair. "Look at where you sit. You have everything. How can you say that I took anything from you?" But he did understand. And his shoulders slumped as he remembered his thoughts from earlier. Besides, they'd get nowhere with that kind of talk. "I'm sorry. I don't begrudge you for disliking me."

"Did you just apologize?"

Ace nodded and pressed his lips together, giving East a direct look. "The truth is, our father did a disservice to both of us."

"How so?"

Ace stared at his hands as he thought about what to say next. "Neither of us got all of him. And I'm guessing none of us got what we needed."

East was silent as Ace lifted his head to study the other man. "That's what my wife says as well."

His wife.

Marriage.

He'd heard of East's nuptials at the club. But the details had been vague at best, an oddity in and of itself that Ace had puzzled over at the time. A lord's marriage was usually an event of much conversation. "Congratulations."

East gave him an odd look. "I suppose you are one of the few people who could celebrate the nuptials without judgment."

His brows drew together in confusion. "I'm sorry?"

East shook his head. "My wife is the bastard sister of the Duke of Devonshire."

Surprise rocked through him. His brother had had nothing to do with any of his siblings but he married a bastard? Did that even make sense? "You're not jesting?"

East gave him a level stare. "I fell in love."

Love. Sounded simple enough. Was it that easy?

East pushed the money across the table. Surely it was enough to sustain them for some time. But it wasn't close to enough to transform the club the way he wished. The place needed new floors, new furnishings, more staff. And he still needed to support his family. "This terminates your partnership at the Den of Sins."

Ace cleared his throat. He still hadn't asked for what he came for in the first place. "I understand. But I hoped to ask for something else."

East grimaced. "What?"

His mouth twitched. Asking for financial statements didn't exactly make him look innocent if East thought him in league with thieves. "I want to build up Hell's Corner, but I need partners for that."

"I'll not work with you again."

Ace shook his head. "I've asked other men but they want to know the revenue potential. If I could share some information from the Den of Sins—"

"No." East stood and fisted his hands at his sides.

"No?"

"I've been more than generous. The money in that bag not only terminates our partnership but our relationship."

Ace's lip curled in distaste. "Your wife. Was she well off before you married her?"

East gave him a questioning glare. "What does that have to do with anything?"

"You have two half-sisters, you know. Two half-sisters who'd like to marry someday. Have families of their own. They don't need to marry lords but I'm trying to provide humble dowries for them. Some chance at a future. I get that you don't like me, perhaps you hate our brothers too. But Mirabelle and Anna are two of the sweetest girls and they need help." More words bubbled to the surface. So odd. He never overshared.

Emotions long bottled were pushing their way through and if he didn't stop now, they might all come spilling out.

He clamped his lips shut. He was about to lose his pride in addition to the possibility of failing his family after all.

East opened his mouth, his face creased as though Ace's words had caused him pain. Or perhaps that was just anger over the past. More likely, it was the latter.

With that thought, he spun on heel and stormed out the door. His past with East was too raw to move forward into the future. He'd have to find another way.

CHAPTER SEVEN

THE NEXT AFTERNOON, Emily stood near the entrance of Hyde Park, her footman stationed next to her as per her brother's instructions.

She'd not been able to slip away and meet Mirabelle without a servant in attendance as she might have a week ago.

Lord Smith's attention had her brother's watchful gaze trained directly at Emily. Her brother had lectured her for a solid quarter hour the day before about accepting a ride from Lord Smith when their own carriage was on its way to the orphanage.

She'd nodded and said little.

Again, words failed her. She ought to have told him how she'd just made a mistake. Though, she hadn't.

Or perhaps she should have stood up and declared her romantic feelings for Lord Smith. Feelings no man had matched. Should she have demanded her right to choose her future? Not that she wanted to choose Lord Smith. He'd hurt her yesterday with his declaration she ought to marry Somersworth.

But still. She should have some say in her own path. It was her right.

While she had a dowry that was under her brother's control, she also had a significant inheritance from her mother, money that Emily could live off comfortably for the rest of her life.

But she hadn't reminded him of that either. Instead, she'd listened attentively as he'd lectured her about the carriage ride and then he'd left with Upton and Somersworth to go who knows where.

Their gentleman's club? Their boxing club? Somewhere even more interesting?

It all seemed unfair. She wasn't even allowed to go to the park, for heaven's sake.

Mirabelle's family carriage came into sight, pulling off to the side to unload its passengers.

But Mirabelle wasn't the first person to step from the vehicle. Lord Smith ducked out the door, large and imposing, and stealing her breath in an instant.

Emily cursed herself. She didn't want to like him.

A second gentleman stepped out of the carriage looking a great deal like Lord Smith, albeit a younger version.

Same brown hair, same broad shoulders.

He handed out Mirabelle and the three of them started toward Emily as she reminded herself to breathe.

Mirabelle waved as the footman cleared his throat. "Did Baron Boxby know you were having an outing with mixed company?"

"I didn't know," she replied, in a whisper. She hadn't. She'd expected this meeting to be with Mirabelle. Of course, she'd known that the family didn't have servants, hence why Mirabelle's brothers squired her everywhere. Why did one of them have to be Ace?

"Emily." Mirabelle waved again. "You came."

"Of course, I did." Emily gave a falsely bright smile, nerves fluttering in her belly. Not only was Ace causing the riot in her stomach but she'd lied to Mirabelle yesterday, a falsehood her brother had uncovered when he'd called her out in front of their townhouse yesterday. Emily winced at the memory. Was Mirabelle upset?

As the tall brunette moved closer, she unhooked her hand from her escort's arms and held out her hands to Emily. "I'm so glad to see you."

"I'm glad too," Emily replied, clasping Mirabelle's hands.

"This is my brother, Lord Rushton," Mirabelle said and then looked back. "Rush, this is Miss Boxby."

"Pleasure," he said with a quick jerk of his chin.

Mirabelle gave her fingers a squeeze and then linked her arm with Emily's, starting down the wide path. It was early in the day, not yet two in the afternoon, and well before the fashionable time, so the paths were fairly clear of other people as they made their way through the park. Leaves rustled crisply in the breeze, the fall air crisp and cool as they walked.

She looked back to see Lord Smith, Lord Rush, and her footman trailing behind.

"Sorry I had to bring them," Mirabelle whispered close to her ear. "Something happened yesterday that has all my brothers worried. They of course won't tell me what the precise event was that has them so concerned. But when I told them I'd help they asked me how and then I told them about your promise and now..." Mirabelle looked back too. "I'm not sure why they're here. But they insisted on coming. Both of them."

Emily shook her head. "Please don't apologize. It's me who should be saying sorry to you. Yesterday, I didn't tell you the truth—"

Mirabelle waved her hand. "Don't give it another thought." Then she leaned close again. "You wanted to see Ace again, didn't you?"

Emily couldn't deny it. She gave a quick nod.

Mirabelle bounced on her heels. "Oh that is exciting. Unless..." And then her friend stopped. "You plan to allow the earl to court you after all."

Emily shook her head. "I don't know what I plan other than convincing my brother to allow me to invite you all for dinner."

Mirabelle gave her a sympathetic look. "Ace didn't make it any easier, did he? I've never seen him act like that before."

"Like what?"

Mirabelle raised a shoulder. "He seemed angry and a bit sullen when you were in the carriage with us. He's frequently quiet but usually kind."

Emily lifted her brows. He'd been a bit irritated since the moment she'd met him, not that it had stopped her from finding him attractive. Odd how that worked. "He's likely just worried about your family. I'll speak to my brother about that dinner invitation tonight."

Mirabelle nodded.

"Mira," Rush called from behind them. "Come look at this bird. Do you know what kind it is?"

Mirabelle gave her brother a questioning glance as she loosened her hold on Emily's arm and slowed her step to pivot and make her way back to her brother's side.

Ace instantly took Mirabelle's spot.

"Good afternoon, Miss Boxby."

"Lord Smith," she said, her back stiffening as he held out his elbow. She hesitated for a moment before she slipped her hand into his arm. Her gloved fingers settled into the heat that radiated out of his jacket as he started them walking again.

"How was your evening?" he asked.

"Uneventful," she answered, swallowing a lump. She didn't want to spend time with this man. Not after he'd made his lack of interest completely clear. And yet, she couldn't seem to stop her wayward body from enjoying the thrill of excitement that coursed through her at his touch. "And yours?"

"Very eventful."

She gasped in surprise, her chin snapping up so that she might look in his eyes. "What happened?"

He frowned. "The details are for another time. If you'd allow me to move straight to the point, Mirabelle and Anna need me to succeed at the business venture I've started. It's imperative. I've asked your brother to aid me in my endeavor, but he is...uncertain."

She nodded, understanding. Was he asking for her help? "I already told Mirabelle I'll talk to my brother tonight about a dinner invitation. I meant to speak with him yesterday, but our time together last night was mostly spent with me listening and him talking."

"About me?"

She pressed her lips together as she ducked her head so that he didn't see the confirmation in her features. The fall breeze fluttered the ribbons of her bonnet even as leaves swirled about them adding a romantic whimsy to the afternoon. She frowned as they danced about her. She did not wish to be swept away by fancy just now.

"He doesn't approve of me, as well he shouldn't," Ace said with a quiet certainty that had her chin lifting again. "And I apologize if I sounded harsh yesterday. I didn't intend to. I just…"

Chills ran down her spine as she held her breath and wondered what he might say next.

———

ACE PLACED his other hand over her small fingers tucked in his elbow. He'd like to tell her everything. That he'd attempted to push her away because she was breaking through all of his carefully constructed barriers. She'd started on their very first meeting and each time he looked into the warm pools of her eyes, he sank a little deeper in, and a bit more of his resistance melted away.

Which likely made this plan a bad idea.

He shouldn't be walking with her like this. Shouldn't be telling her that he'd been too hard. She *should* think of him as too hard, too impenetrable, and then she should marry another man.

But he hated that idea too.

Though to be fair he also hated what he was about to do almost as much, which was to ask Emily for help.

A woman like her should be protected. Not burdened.

But with East cutting him off, Ace had to find another path to help his brothers and sisters. And the only one forward was next to Emily.

"You were just what?" she asked, sounding breathless.

"I just think I'm no good for you."

"Oh," she whispered so softly, he almost didn't hear it. "But the Earl of Somersworth would be?"

Ace grimaced, hating the next words. "He has money, power, a legitimate title. He could care for you."

Emily nodded, looking down the path. Then she looked back at him again. "There is only one problem. He doesn't make my heart flutter wildly in my chest." And then she blushed.

Ace had already known, of course, that she was attracted to him. But her words... The admission that Ace made her heart flutter in her chest had every fiber of his body clenching in response. He wanted to kiss her.

He wanted to hold her in his arms. The rest of the world could hang.

Mirabelle's laughter floated up to him and he closed his eyes, remembering why he cared about the rest of the world after all. Or at least his little corner of it. "I can't give you the life you're accustomed. The life you deserve."

"I don't care about any of that."

He shook his head. She didn't care now because she had every opportunity at her disposal. But would she think differently if she was tied to a man who couldn't give her what she'd been accustomed to? "I have to do what's best for my siblings, Emily. They need me to succeed, which is why I need your brother as an ally. I can't anger him by courting you."

Her face fell, her lips pulling down and then trembling. "I...I see."

"Mirabelle and my other siblings count on me." He didn't know why he explained other than he wanted her to understand. Somehow, he felt like he owed her that.

She nodded. "I care about Mirabelle too." She drew in a long breath. "Why don't you come for dinner on Friday? I'll make certain my brother is in attendance and that he's receptive to hearing about your plan for the gaming hell."

His brows lifted. It's what he'd hoped for, but now that he'd reached his goal, he didn't like it one bit. He was the sort of man who cared for a woman, not the other way around. "I'll convince your brother without your help, Emily. You should attend your own future. Not mine."

"I'm attending Mirabelle's too," she said with a small smile that didn't reach her eyes. "And mine is already decided, no? I can just marry the earl. Done. Easy."

49

She'd not repeated those word until this moment, at least not to Ace, and he realized he despised them on her lips. He liked it far better when she was denying she'd consider the Earl of Somersworth. "Easy."

She gave a quick nod as they stopped to wait for Mirabelle and Rush.

"I mean it, Emily, you needn't intercede on my behalf. I'll see my family through. I always do."

She didn't answer as she looked at Mirabelle. He wanted to ask what she was thinking but he wasn't certain he had the right.

The rest of the outing passed without any more private conversation between them, though Ace found he couldn't tear his gaze from her. Her eyes sparkled, her smile warmed his insides, and the gentle sway of her body stole his breath.

He found himself wondering if there might be another way...a way to provide for his family and make Emily his. Because the more he looked at her, the more he knew he couldn't give her up without at least trying.

CHAPTER EIGHT

EMILY CLASPED her hands as she waited outside her brother's study.

He'd been talking with Upton and Somersworth for more than an hour and she'd heard the distinct clink of crystal. They were drinking.

She wondered if he'd receive her request with more or less irritation for having partaken in some brandy?

There was only one way to find out.

She took several deep breaths.

She'd hoped the other two men would leave but they'd not, and she didn't wish to put the request off any longer.

She was nervous enough as it was. She pressed her palms to her dress, hoping to remove some of the clamminess before she raised her hand to knock on the door.

Why she grew nervous to speak with her brother, she couldn't say. He loved her. But her insides didn't agree. Any negative emotion sent her into a flustered babbling mess.

And worse than asking in front of just her brother would be to ask in front of other people.

She thought of Somersworth. What would he think? Would this further fuel his interest or push him away? She hoped the latter. Much as she'd always wished to marry, she'd realized an important fact about herself. She wished to marry, not just for the sake of the institution, but for love.

And she'd not be able to settle for less.

Which was the thought that seemed to finally push her to raise her hand and rap on the door.

"Yes?" her brother asked.

She cracked open the door. "Ken. I'd like to speak with you."

"Come in," he said and she pushed the door open further, stepping into the room. Ken sat on the other side of the desk, his feet propped on the top while both Upton and Somersworth sat in chairs between the desk and the door.

The fire crackled merrily in the hearth as the faint scent of smoke and liquor added an atmosphere of warmth.

All the men stood as she entered the room, Somersworth setting his glass aside and stepping up next to her.

Ken looked between the two of them, his gaze narrowing. She shifted, her breath trembling out of her lungs. The last thing this conversation needed was another complication. Had Lord Somersworth told Ken about his admission at the ball? Did Ken approve? Did it matter?

"I need a few minutes with my sister," Ken said as Upton started to file past her toward the paneled door. But Somersworth paused, his hand brushing hers. "Remember what I said."

"I haven't forgotten," she answered, her gaze pointed down to her toes. He'd be the next person she'd have to find the courage to tell the truth. He slid past her and out the door, it softly clicking closed.

Silence filled the room as she slowly raised her gaze to her brother's. He stared back at her, one lock of his wavy brown hair falling over his forehead. He brushed it back with a quick hand. "What is going on?"

"What do you mean?" she asked her brows rising.

"First Smith and now Somersworth. Why was he looking at you like that?"

That made her smile. "I thought you wanted me to have suitors."

His eyes narrowed into slits. "Neither of them are appropriate choices for you."

"An earl and the second son of a marquess are not appropriate?" She cocked her head to the side assessing her brother. She'd assumed he was eager for her to be a success. That he was embarrassed by her lack of progress. Had she gotten that wrong?

Ken's mouth opened and then closed again. "Somersworth's reputation is—"

"The same as yours."

Ken's mouth snapped shut. "And Smith is..." But he trailed off.

"What is he?"

"There are rumors."

Emily shook her head. "Since when do you listen to rumors?" She knew that he referred to the fact that Ace was actually a bastard. It wasn't rumor, it was fact. But that didn't mean that Ace was less. At least not to her.

"I listen when they involve the happiness of my sister," Ken fired back.

Emily shook her head. "The rumors have little to do with whether or not he'd make me happy."

"I disagree. If he's the imposter they say he is—" Ken stopped, his lips pressing into a thin line.

"Ken." She took in a deep breath, choosing her words carefully rather than prattling on nervously. This was important. "Anyone can see that everything Lord Smith does is for the protection of his family."

"And what if he wants to marry you for the protection of his family? Would that make you happy? To be used for your dowry?"

Heat flooded her face as she winced in pain. "Rest assured. He doesn't wish to marry me."

"How do you know that?"

She shrugged, her fingers twisting together. "He told me. But he does need help so that he might provide for Mirabelle and so I need—"

"Mirabelle."

"To ask you to see him again. Perhaps for dinner. This Friday."

Ken's brows lifted. "You want to have him here?"

"I do."

"But not because you wish to pursue a courtship with him?"

She tried to keep her face free of emotion as she gave a quick nod. For once, she hadn't allowed her words to run away with her or clammed up with nervousness. She'd not ruin it now.

"That's right," she said. "I wish to help Mirabelle. She's a lovely girl who deserves a future."

Ken let out a long sigh. "Fine. I'll invite him to dinner on Friday night."

She stepped closer, relief making her shoulders limp. "And you'll consider his proposal?"

"What do you know about that?" Ken said, the volume of his voice rising with every word. Clearly she'd found another point of irritation.

She took a half step back, her pulse beginning to thrum. "Just what Mirabelle told me."

"And what does she know?"

Emily took several more breaths as her fingers pressed to her stomach. This was Ken. He loved her. Why did she allow her nerves to scramble her reasoning? "Just that her brother's business is necessary to keep the family financially stable. He wants to provide dowries for his sisters and incomes for his four brothers."

Ken waved his hand. "Fine. I'll listen. Are you happy?"

"Yes."

"And Emily." Ken moved around the desk. "If Somersworth makes any more overtures, you tell me. I don't care that you could be a countess, he's not right for you."

Her brows shot up. "Why not? He's your friend."

"He's a rake."

Relief coursed through her, softening her shoulders. "I'll take all you said under consideration, but rest assured, I'm not interested in Somersworth."

"Good." Then he cocked his head. "Why?"

She shrugged. "I just don't feel any affection for him beyond what I feel for any of your friends."

Her brother nodded. "Trust your instincts then."

She would. And she was glad to have helped Ace like this. What came next for her, she had no idea. But as she left, she hurried down the hall to write to Mirabelle and tell her that her plan had been successful.

Which meant she'd be having dinner with Ace in two days' time. She inwardly sighed. Every time she saw him, she fell a bit more in love.

Would this dinner be an opportunity to convince him that he ought to consider a future with her? Her breath caught as she slowed her steps. That was what she wished for more than anything.

———

EMILY HAD DONE IT. She'd secured a second meeting with the baron. What was more, the note he'd received from Baron Boxby indicated he was going to support Hell's Corner.

Gratitude swelled in Ace's chest.

Not only did the woman fill him with warmth but now she'd made his life that much easier.

This feeling was such a rarity, he swiped a hand down his face. She had melted his resistance before. Now…

Ace stood outside Baron Boxby's townhouse and waited for the butler to open the door.

He had to find a way to place some sort of barrier between them. Her future depended on it.

Much as he'd tried to think of a way for the two of them to be together, he'd not come up with an answer.

He lived a lie. One that might land him in prison at any moment. Especially with the number of people who knew the truth mounting.

It was enough that he got the business established before the truth was discovered by the crown. There would be no future for him once he was tossed in the Tower.

He couldn't embroil Emily in his mess. It wasn't fair to her. But damn, did he want to hold her close and never let her go.

The door opened and he shook off his thoughts, stepping inside. Those worries were for later. Right now, he needed to finish what he'd set out to do.

The butler led him to the sitting room where both Emily and Baron Boxby waited. The sight of her made his gut twist, a lump rising in his throat.

She appeared the picture of serenity tonight. Her pale blue silk dress, conservative in its neckline, still highlighted her delicate frame. And that smile... There was no outward sign of the insecurity she'd expressed the first time he'd met her. It was like watching a flower bloom before his very eyes.

He swallowed the lump down, bowing to the baron as they said their hellos.

"Good of you to have me," he said looking from Emily to her brother.

The baron gave a slight smile. "My sister insisted."

His gaze swung back to Emily, her gaze soft and understanding. "My brother exaggerates."

Boxby surely hadn't.

They sat and Boxby gave him a long, appraising stare. "Forgive me for asking, but I'm unfamiliar with your family tree."

Ace had all the answers to the questions Boxby was about to ask, but why the baron was asking was another matter entirely. He knew Ace was a bastard and a liar. Did he hope to protect his sister by digging into Ace? Figure out more about Ace as a business partner? Expose his lies to Emily so she ceased to be interested? "Not surprising. Both my father and eldest brother suffer from terrible gout and don't travel much."

"You have an older brother, of course. The heir."

He didn't. Well, that is to say that the Marquess of Highgrove did have an heir who suffered from gout. They were his father's cousins. And neither man had been to London in well over twenty years.

Between their decrepit finances and their sickly conditions, they'd be unlikely to make the journey anytime soon.

It was a perfect cover for his fake title. Until they both died and the marquessate fell to East. Then everyone would know that Ace was a fraud and a liar.

"I do." He gave Boxby a level stare.

"Funny. You carry yourself like you could be the eldest."

Because he was. But he shrugged. These lies came easily to him. "My father and brother are both sickly."

Boxby gave a quick nod of understanding. "And the finances."

"Poor. Hence why I'm here."

"And that's why your home is in Cheapside?"

There were fashionable neighborhoods in London. And as the supposed son of a marquess, he ought to live in one of them. "The family home was sold years ago." A truth. "The home my family resides in now was the one I could afford to purchase." Somewhat true.

"And all your other siblings came with you?"

Ace drew in a deep breath. He should have expected this questioning. But he'd been distracted by thoughts of Emily. He looked at her now, her eyes brimming with worry. Was she concerned for him? He deserved this interrogation and far, far worse. "The best opportunities are here. For my brothers, they can make money and my sisters…"

Boxby finally softened, his features relaxing as his shoulders lost their tension. "They'll make the best matches here."

Ace nodded.

Emily pressed invisible wrinkles out of her skirt as she leaned forward in her seat. "Speaking of, tell us of your other sister, Anna. We've not had the pleasure of meeting."

He did as she asked. Anna was the only blonde in his family and she was secretly the light in all their hearts. At seventeen, she still held touches of childhood that often made Ace smile and reminded him why all his hard work was worth the trouble. He knew his affection for his youngest sister shone through, but it wasn't only her that he appreciated.

Emily had intentionally steered the topic of conversation to safer waters for his benefit. A gentle smile played at her lips as she listened to his description of Anna with rapt attention. He wanted to introduce Emily to his Anna. To all his siblings.

They'd like her.

She stole his breath now as she laughed at an anecdote he told about a time Anna had become stuck in a tree she'd climbed. It had taken two brothers to untangle her from the mess.

Boxby laughed too.

And that's when Ace realized Emily had done more than just steer change the subject. She'd brought them to a sympathetic one. Boxby liked hearing about the women in Ace's family.

A relieved breath rushed from his lungs. Ace was winning over the baron.

Thanks to Emily.

Again.

Did she consider herself unable to converse effectively? Not true. She might sometimes speak quickly or say too much but she always talked from her heart. He could see that clearly. Did she?

CHAPTER NINE

DID Ace know that his voice grew deeper when he lied?

Emily could hear it, the way he drew strength from inside when he protected his family with his story.

She supposed it was wrong to admire him for his strength but she couldn't quell the emotion. How far would she go if Ken's wellbeing were hanging in the balance? Very far.

The butler came in to announce dinner and their small party made their way to the dining room, she and Ken walking in front of Ace.

She could feel him behind her. His energy, his strength.

He stole her breath.

She peeked back, catching his eye as a blush filled her cheeks. She shouldn't respond. There was little point to blushing, to the rush of emotion that filled her whenever their gazes met. But the breathless rush of excitement filled her anyway.

He was a fortress of strength. How could she think she'd ever be able to penetrate his defenses and win his heart? In all likelihood, the task was a fool's errand, but she had to try anyway.

Her chin snapped forward again, breaking their eye contact as she held her brother's elbow.

They made their way into the dining room, their conversation continuing as a delicate French vichyssoise was ladled out for the first course.

Her stomach protested. How could she eat when butterflies beat like mad all through her chest and abdomen?

Thankfully, she managed a few bites of the light fare before the next course arrived.

"Emily." Her brother gave her a meaningful stare. "You hardly touched your soup."

A sigh of exasperation rested on her lips as she attempted to hold it in. "Kind of you to notice."

"You're thin enough as it is," he chastised.

Her shoulders straightened. Didn't he realize this was embarrassing? But she clamped her lips shut.

Ace caught her eye, giving her the tiniest wink. The simple gesture made her spine straighten. "Must we discuss my eating habits now?"

Ken grimaced. "You're the one who didn't finish your soup."

She opened her mouth to protest but drew in a fortifying breath. She could tell him how embarrassing all this was or she could say nothing. But as her mind calmed, she found a nice middle. "Lord Smith does not need to hear our nightly bickering."

"Quite right," Ken answered as he continued to frown at her. Quail was set in front of each of them and the conversation moved on until a toe softly tapped her slipper under the table.

Her fork nearly dropped from her hand as Ace winked again. And then the foot gently nudged hers...twice.

A grin played at her lips as she nudged back.

She'd once heard a lady in the repose tell a fascinating tale of a gentleman with wandering hands under the dinner table. It had been a mesmerizing and mildly embarrassing story to a younger Emily. She'd both been a bit appalled a man would do such a thing so publicly and intrigued at the obvious excitement in the woman's voice.

This was not that.

The small touch was meant as a comfort. A way for Ace to offer her support at the tension between her and her brother.

But all the same, she had a moment where she wished...

What would it be like to feel Ace's hand sliding over her skirts and up her leg?

A delicious sensation throbbed at her core. She set down her fork, her hand fluttering to her throat as she considered whether or not she might fan herself because heat was now rising up her body and it would infuse her cheeks soon enough.

Did Ace see it?

His gaze narrowed, his eyes sweeping down her neck.

His gaze felt like a touch and her skin prickled with awareness.

This was exactly what wasn't supposed to happen. She was not supposed to respond to him like this at the dinner table in front of her brother. Was she? She knew so little about how a woman won a man's affection. It had been that inexperience which had propelled her toward him in the first place. But she wished she'd learned more as his heated stare held hers.

She finally looked away, staring down the length of the room to avoid his gaze.

Blessedly, the quail was taken away and the next course served.

She needed to escape this room. Needed to escape his presence.

She paused, her chest tightening in regret. Once she did escape, she might never see Ace again. They had no more cause to be together. Her eyes darted back to his, his still fixed on her.

Did he realize that too? Did he care about not seeing her again?

A wild idea crept into her thoughts. He'd been clear they had no future and she knew she'd be unlikely to change his mind no matter what she did or said, she didn't want their relationship to end.

Not that she usually got what she wished. But while he was here tonight, couldn't she just have one small touch to remember this night? Or perhaps, dare she hope, to propel them forward?

Ignoring the roasted vegetables in front of her as she attempted to think of way to catch him alone. Surely, she could think of something...

———

WHEN THE LAST course was served, Emily left, retiring to the music room, and leaving him and Boxby to converse.

This was why he'd come. This conversation. And yet, he hated to see her go.

Her brother had been right.

She'd barely touched her meal, picking at her food all night. But he'd also seen her features tighten at Boxby's words. She was feeling henpecked by her brother. And her issues with speaking her mind became clearer.

Her brother loved her.

But Boxby smothered her with that affection. Emily needed a bit more room to find herself and her voice.

Not that Ace would bring up any of that. He had his agenda and that was the reason he was here but part of him wished he could advocate for her. She'd helped Ace so much, he'd like to return the favor.

Boxby's voice pulled him out of his reverie. "So, you'd like to discuss the club again."

"That's right." He forced his attention back to the conversation.

"And you used my sister's affection for you to gain this meeting?"

Damn. He should have seen that barb coming. "Your sister has an affection for me?"

Boxby's jaw tightened. "Tell me more about your plans."

He drew in a breath. "They're simple really. The Den of Sins is popular because of its connection with wealth and power. And it amplifies that connection by having lush furniture, posh alcohol, attractive dealers."

Boxby's eyes lit with understanding and he sat up straighter in his chair. "Of course."

"I want to reproduce those results but I need money and better connections to do that."

"And the numbers?"

Ace grimaced. "So far I've not been successful on that front."

Boxby frowned. "Too bad."

Ace rattled off several of the profit margins he knew from being in the club and helping with the count. He could only hope they were enough.

Boxby sat forward in his chair, his attention rapt as Ace shared what he knew. "And what's to stop me from taking this and starting my own club?"

Ace swallowed his growl of protest. "My brothers and I will work the club full time. No effort on your part is required. Will you get that with your own club?"

Boxby gave him an appreciative glance as he rubbed his chin. "All right. You've convinced me. I'm your first partner."

Ace pulled up straighter. He'd done it…

With Emily's help.

"I know that Upton and Somersworth are interested as well. I'll tell them all that you told me, but I think they'll both want numbers."

"Somersworth?"

Boxby raised his brows. "He is one of my closest friends. I know you only approached Upton and myself but…"

Ace waved his hand. "He's exactly the sort we'd be interested in partnering with." He stopped. How did he explain that the idea of having to see Emily with another man was like a dagger to the chest?

"Except?"

Ace pressed his lips together. He didn't dare answer.

Boxby chuckled. "I understand. But rest assured, Somersworth will not marry my sister."

Ace jolted, unable to contain his surprise. "I beg your pardon?"

"You're surprised?"

"He's an earl."

Boxby shook his head. "He's also far too jaded for someone as gentle as my sister."

Ace ought to give a silent prayer of thanks. But as he looked at Boxby, he wondered if any man would be good enough for the baron's sister. "If I might overstep—"

"You may not."

Ace ignored him. "Be careful not to keep your sister too confined. It's tempting. I know. Trust me, I do."

Boxby opened his mouth to answer but then snapped it closed again. "I'll keep that in mind." The man waved his hand for a drink. Immediately a footman came over with a tray holding a decanter and two glasses. "Shall we toast?"

Ace nodded. "Definitely. But first, would you give me a moment?" He just needed a second to himself. His normally ordered thoughts were a jumble of feelings. Somersworth would not marry Emily. Not that he had any chance either, but still.

Knowing that the earl wouldn't have her mattered.

He left the dining room and started down the hall, knowing that he had to stem the flow of feelings coursing through him. They changed nothing.

And he needed his control now more than ever. It was what had gotten him this far and he was so close to completing the task that would secure his family.

But surely his distracted state was the reason that, as he turned a corner, he didn't see a slender beauty standing in front of him until he ran directly into her.

Emily's small hands reached for his biceps as her feet tangled in his.

Automatically, he grabbed her waist, bringing her against him to keep her from falling.

But the moment her body pressed to his, he knew he was lost. She was achingly soft in all the right places and his body clenched in awareness.

He'd been trying to avoid thoughts of Emily. Calm the feelings she brought out in him. Instead, he found himself tangled in her arms.

Would he ever find himself free of the confusion Emily had created in his once clear mind?

Did he wish to be?

CHAPTER TEN

EMILY HAD BEEN HIDING in wait.

But even she hadn't anticipated literally falling into Ace's arms.

Now that she was here however…

His body was lean, and hard, and so strong. His hands circled her waist in the most masculine way. Her pulse thrummed in her veins as she once again remembered her fantasy of his hand sliding up the stocking of her leg.

Need pulsed through her. "Ace," she managed to squeak out.

"I'm sorry. I wasn't watching where I was going."

She shook her head. "The fault was mine. I was hoping…" Her words trailed off as his features darkened. Was he angry with her?

Fortunately, he didn't push her away. If anything, he pulled her closer. She could feel the brush of his firm stomach against hers. She'd worn a short corset this evening and thank the heavens she had. She bent out, arching her back, to look up at him, their torsos still pressed together and his face grew darker still.

"Emily," he said.

His voice had a rough, gravelly quality that only seemed to make her more aware of everything as her lips parted to speak.

But she couldn't get the words out. No surprise there. Instead, she licked her lips, parched as they were, as she tried to formulate an explanation.

His eyes narrowed as he stared at her mouth. "Emily. I'm going to kiss you."

"Oh. Yes, please," she replied, both eager and grateful no explanation had been required.

The smallest smile ghosted across his mouth before it was gone and he was lowering his lips to hers.

The light brush against her mouth sent waves of sensation rocking through her and she gasped, breathing in the scent of him.

Sandalwood, brandy, cigar, and deep masculine scent mingled together to make a smell as intoxicating as the rest of him. She melted deeper into him as his lips passed over hers again. This time, she kissed back, her hands tightening on his biceps.

She felt him groan and a wave of power like she'd never known surged through her. This was what it was like to be confident. Wanted.

He kissed her again and she eagerly returned the gesture, her fingers sliding up his arms to twine about his neck.

By the fourth press, her body was molded to his, their breath mingled, their eyes locked.

And then he tilted her lips open and dipped his tongue between her lips to taste her.

Emily had never imagined anything so divine and yet so devilish. With a certainty, she knew that this kiss…this was a beginning.

When his tongue dipped into her mouth again, she did some tasting of her own. He was delicious.

But the swipe of her tongue caused his arm to slide about her back, locking her against his chest. "Emily," he groaned as he pulled back just far enough to speak. "What have you done to me?"

"Bewitched you?" she asked hopefully before his mouth dropped over hers again.

Wouldn't it be lovely to make a man this handsome, this mesmerizing, her very own husband one day? But he didn't answer as he plundered her mouth again. And for once, she didn't care about words at all as her lips did something far more interesting and more fun than talk.

Their tongues came together, their lips tasting and nibbling until Emily was so breathless with want, she forgot everything around her.

And when he slid one of his hands from her back, down her backside to cup her cheek and pull her hips into the cradle of his, Emily knew with absolute certainty that she'd never touch another man again.

This one was made for her.

"We have to stop before we're found," he whispered against her mouth in between kisses. "Emily. We can't."

"I don't want to stop," she answered honestly. "I've wanted to kiss you since the first day I met you."

"Me too," he said as he shuffled them closer to the wall, hiding in the shadows of the candlelight.

"I don't want anyone else," she said against his mouth, not even sure he could understand her. "I only want you."

Should she have been so honest? She'd lost any perspective she'd gained over the past weeks as the truth tumbled from her lips.

He didn't respond but the kiss slowly grew less heated, slower, until finally, he stopped all together, lifting his head. "Emily. Try to understand. I'd be selfish to take you for my own."

"Selfish? But we both—"

He kissed her quiet. "I don't have a future. Just a limited amount of time to see the people I love cared for. If I married you, I'd rob you of your future too."

She gasped in a breath as sadness filled her chest. "Oh."

"Understand, Emily. It's because I care that I have to leave you for someone else." And then he eased back, leaving her slumped against the wall, her heart aching even more in her chest.

———

ACE HAD MADE A TERRIBLE MISTAKE.

Emily's kiss hadn't been virginal. It hadn't even been sweet. It had been pure unadulterated fire.

And it had burned him to the core.

Had he pictured pleasant nights spent wrapped in loving arms of warmth and sympathy? Now those fantasies took on a new dimension. Emily wrapped around him, their breath and mouths mingled as they both chased pleasure—

He made his thoughts stop as he halted just outside the dining room. He had to go converse pleasantly with her brother.

He couldn't be fantasizing about all the carnal pleasure Emily's embrace surely held.

For a wild moment he dreamed of carrying her away. They could both disappear.

But his family.

And hers.

Boxby loved his sister with all the brotherly care that Ace felt for Mirabelle and Anna. To steal that away.

He couldn't do it.

He let out a frustrated growl, combed back his hair, and then stepped into the dining room.

But Boxby no longer sat at the table. Instead, he stood at one end of the room near the buffet. Something was wrong. Had the baron seen Ace's and Emily's embrace?

"Smith," Boxby called. "A missive has arrived here for you."

"A missive for me?"

"It's sealed by the Earl of Easton. Apparently, it was delivered to your residence with a message from the earl that this was of great importance, so your brother escorted the delivering footman here." Boxby held out a sealed note.

His brother? Crossing the room in a few long strides, he took the letter from the baron and sliced open the seal, quickly scanning the contents.

He was needed at the Den of Sins. As soon as possible. Making multiple decisions in the span of a breath, Ace looked up at the baron. "Want to see the Den of Sins for yourself?"

Boxby's brows lifted but then he gave a quick nod. "Yes."

"Get your jacket."

Within fifteen minutes, they'd made their way out the door and into Ace's carriage as the vehicle sped across town. Boxby said little, for which Ace was grateful. Between memories of Emily and wonderings about his half-brother and the Den of Sins, his mind was full. What did his brother need from him?

Why would he call on Ace now?

The carriage pulled into the back alley, his driver familiar with the location and the procedure.

Ace entered through the back, moving past the offices. East was not in his, so he and Boxby continued into the front room.

He heard Boxby's rush of breath as they entered, the lighting dim but still gleaming off the highly polished tables. The club was filling quickly, the tables having several guests each.

Crystal glasses winked with a rainbow of liquids from dark red to bubbling gold champagne and quiet laughter added to the ambiance of the room. "The Den of Sins," Ace said as he looked back at Boxby. "Would you care to join a table while I find out what East needs?"

Boxby gave him a sidelong glance. "I don't get to attend your meeting?"

Ace raised a brow. Boxby would not meet with Ace's legitimate brother. "I'm afraid not."

Boxby grimaced. "And here I thought we were becoming friends."

"We are business partners. A relationship I take seriously."

"Do you?" East asked joining them from Ace's left.

Ace knew that his brother suspected Ace was part of the thefts but he'd never partake in such activities. Even he had his limits. He looked at his brother, hiding his glower. "East. Always a pleasure."

"And you, Ace." East's gaze narrowed. "Baron Boxby. Nice to see you again."

"And you," Boxby replied.

"How do you know Lord Smith?"

Boxby cleared his throat. "I'm buying into Hell's Corner."

East cocked his head to the side. "Is that right?"

Ace drew in a long slow breath. What did East think of all this? Ace didn't want his brother's opinion to matter, but somehow, what the other man thought of him did. Emily had surely opened some emotional tap that he now couldn't seem to turn off. "I told you, East. I need Hell's Corner to be a success."

"I know." East gave a quick nod. "That's part of the reason I've asked you here."

That surprised him and his chin pulled back as his lips parted. "Really? There isn't an emergency?"

East looked at Boxby before his gaze settled back on Ace. "Apologies if I led you to believe something was amiss. I only wished you to come quickly because I realized I had erred and…" The other man paused with a slight wince. "Since he's your partner, I can share this in front of him. I'd like to buy shares in Hell's Corner as well."

Ace swallowed his lump of surprise. East had just removed him from the Den of Sins. Why would he wish to take part in Hell's Corner?

"Excellent," Boxby crowed. "When I tell Upton and Somersworth, they are sure to join as well."

"Somersworth? We've got an earl already," Ace replied before he'd thought the words through. What had gotten into him? But he already knew. He could swear that the longer he knew Emily, the more like her he became. Sharing his feelings about Somersworth unguarded. He ought to be worried about why his brother had taken a sudden interest in his club. Did East intend him or his siblings harm?

Boxby only chuckled. "In this he'll be a good partner, and I already told you, he'll not marry Emily."

East's brows raised. "Emily?"

Bloody hell. Was he going to have to explain how he'd fallen in love with a woman of the peerage?

Boxby rolled his eyes. "Ace is infatuated with my sister."

And now they were talking about him like he wasn't even there.

"Really?" East asked with a grin. "And will he win her?"

Boxby's look of amusement turned dark in an instant. "No."

East raised his brows. "I see." And then he gestured Ace forward. "Come. We've other business to discuss. Boxby, enjoy the club."

Ace followed, wondering about Emily and Hell's Corner in equal measures. Of course, Emily would never be Ace's but the constant reminder cut him to the bone.

And what did East want from Ace's club?

But he shook his head, shaking off his disappointment as he looked at his brother's back. He needed to focus as he readied himself for the discussion ahead.

CHAPTER ELEVEN

ACE'S QUESTION was answered soon enough.

He entered East's office and his brother immediately handed him a packet of papers. A brief glance revealed they were the very documents he'd requested during their last meeting. "What?" he began, but realized it was the wrong question. He shook his head. "Why?"

East shrugged, his gaze casting down. "My wife, for starters. Her legitimate brothers have welcomed her with open arms and..." East face spasmed as his gaze lifted to Ace's. "I want to help care for our sisters."

Ace blinked in surprise, the air whooshing from his lungs. A relief he hadn't imagined possible coursed through him. "The rest of...my brothers...our brothers, they can all take care of themselves, but Mirabelle and Anna—"

"You've already convinced me," East said softly. "I'm financing Hell's Corner to help you secure their futures."

Ace nodded. "Thank you."

"Now tell me about Miss Cross."

His head snapped up, that weight returning. "There's nothing to tell. You heard Boxby. He'll not allow me to court her. There are too many rumors about my legitimacy."

East's brows lifted. "Protective of his sister?"

"Very."

"And does she feel the same about you?"

Pain throbbed in his chest. "She does. Not that it matters. My hands are tied."

"Why is that? You'd not work around Boxby in some fashion or another?"

He shrugged. "I'd not come between family."

East studied him, his head turning a bit to the side. "Truly?"

"You'll understand someday."

"I'm sure I will," East answered, but he looked at Ace in a way he never had before. Like, perhaps he finally understood him or maybe he just trusted his bastard brother a bit more. Ace was grateful for his brother's acceptance.

What was more, he'd gotten what he'd wished for. A future for his family.

But the victory was far more hollow than he'd imagined possible. Without Emily... He looked down at the papers in his hand. "Thank you again."

East stepped a bit closer. "You're welcome, though I should tell you, they come with a stipulation."

"What's that?" Unease skittered along his skin as he straightened, looking at his half-brother.

"I want..." East drew in a breath. "I want to meet them. Our sisters."

Surprise made his eyes grow wide. "Really?"

East nodded. "You were right about something else. I thought he'd given most of his money to you so I've been combing through the books. Turns out, he just squandered much of it. Our father liked an extravagant life and we all paid the price for that, didn't we?"

Clearly, East had realized that Ace had told the truth on multiple fronts. Was that why his half-brother was trusting him for the first time? "We did."

It was an odd truce. East was the man who had the potential to cause Ace the most harm. When the current marquess died, it was East who'd likely expose the falsehood of Ace's claim to legitimacy.

Not that he begrudged East taking the title that was rightfully his. "Just promise me that no matter what happens to me, Mirabelle and Anna will be cared for."

"What happens to you?" East asked. "What might happen…" But his words tapered off as a yell sounded through the club.

Then a scream. And another.

The sound of a near stampede thundered down the hall, yells and cries filling the small space.

"Fire," a man's voice boomed from the gaming room.

Ace turned and wrenched open the door, smoke pouring into the room.

"We've got to get out of here," East yelled, pushing at Ace's back.

They made a break for the back, joining the mass of people trying to get out the door as several more screams filled the night. The smoke was so thick that they could hardly see the floor in front of them as Ace made his way down the hall, East's hands on his shoulders. "Don't let go." He called behind him, ducking lower to attempt to avoid the smoke.

"I won't," East said, tightening his grip.

Suddenly, the other man fell into Ace's back. "East?" Ace looked over his shoulder again.

"I've tripped on something!" East called and Ace spun, squinting into the smoke. Curled on the floor was a person.

Without thought, he pushed East to the side, bending down to lift the body up. Lighter than he'd imagined, he knew instantly it was a woman.

"Arabella?" he asked, even as he turned and started for the door once again. Arabella, a partner at the club was one of the only ladies who might be here.

She was also East's very good friend.

"Arabella?" East croaked behind him as they reached the door and lurched out into the fresh air of the night.

It was her. Unconscious in his arms.

"Arabella," East cried, gasping in a breath.

Ace dropped to his knees, and resting Arabella on his thighs, he thumped on her chest several times. Was she breathing?

She let out a coughing, gasping breath, her lungs heaving as her unfocused eyes blinked and her body spasmed.

He held her head up, not knowing what else to do as East dropped down next to him.

"I'm all right," she croaked out. "Someone knocked me down, I think." She swiped her strawberry blonde hair back from her sooty face.

"Where is Edge?" East asked, wiping more of the grime from her cheeks and chin.

"I don't know," she said.

"We have to find him." East gently took Arabella into his own arms, standing with her as he did.

Boxby ran up to them. "Bloody hell, is everyone all right?"

But Ace didn't answer. A movement in the shadows caught his gaze. It looked to be a man. Odd. Why wouldn't that man be helping as people poured from the club? "Boxby," he whispered. "Did you see that?"

Boxby followed his gaze. "See what?"

"A man, there," Ace didn't point but he gave his chin a quick jerk. "Why is he hiding?"

But it was East who answered. "I don't know, but go. Follow him."

Ace gave a quick nod of assent as he melted into the shadows too, Boxby just behind him as he moved into the alley.

He stopped again, searching the night and just caught sight of a man further down the alley slipping to the right.

Holding a finger up to his mouth, he followed, his steps as stealthy as he could make them as they moved down alley after alley.

Boxby didn't say a word and he kept his steps just as quiet as the two men worked through the shadows, moving deeper into the east end of London until they found themselves at the docks of the Thames.

Standing on the other side of the corner, Ace watched as the man knocked on a side door and entered a warehouse.

Where were they?

"Look there," Boxby whispered. "There's a window."

His eyes scanned the side of the building where Boxby pointed. "It's ten feet up at least," Ace answered with a frown.

"Who's standing on whose shoulders?"

He looked over at Boxby, not a small man but a little smaller than Ace. His gaze swept the alley. "Fortunately, neither. Are those some crates over there?"

As quickly as they dared, they picked one up and set it silently down under the window, climbing up on top of the box and standing on the balls of their feet. Ace could just see inside. And what he saw left him cold.

There had to be a hundred men. And above them all was one standing with his arms crossed. Slight, he had the hard stare of a man in charge. "The commander," Ace whispered, awe filling his throat. Bloody hell.

"What?" Boxby asked giving his shoulder a slight push. "Or who is that?"

He looked at Boxby trying to concisely explain. "The Den of Sins, and many other clubs, have been plagued by thieves for months. But a month ago, we caught the commander's brother and sent him to the Tower."

"Shit."

While several of the men inside the warehouse moved crates, at least ten of them sat counting piles of coin. Clearly their thieving had proved lucrative. And with the Den of Sins' owners closing in on the thieves, the thieves had decided to retaliate.

"What just happened at the club was retribution."

"How do you know?" Boxby asked.

"An educated guess." He scrubbed at his jaw. "As a man came straight from there to here, he'd been directed to set that fire." Ace was looking at the possible center of their operation. They'd been chasing this man for months.

And Ace had been the one to find him—and only because of that fire.

"I'd say that's a pretty safe guess. But how are you going to fight so many men?"

They weren't. Not alone.

"Remember the address. We need help."

Boxby nodded. "Done."

Climbing down from the crate, they carefully returned it to its former spot and then started back toward the Den of Sins. What happened next was East's decision not Ace's. But he'd tell his brother everything.

———

EMILY TRIED to wait up for Ken, but hours passed with no sign of him. Where had he gone with Ace that he was out so late?

Sitting in the front parlor, her head propped under her arms on the windowsill, she stared out into the night.

She finally slipped into sleep only to wake suddenly at the sound of carriage wheels breaking the silence.

Jolting up, she watched her brother climb from Ace's carriage, Ace stepping out too. His face was cast in shadow but everything about his body seemed coiled, tense. Was everything all right? She wished she could hold him close, ask what was wrong.

Her brother gave Ace a pat on the back before he turned and started inside. Ace climbed back in his carriage, the vehicle rolling away. What had happened?

She jumped from her seat, racing out the door and down the stairs to meet her brother at the door.

The moment he saw her, he stopped. "What are you doing up?"

Her mouth opened and then closed. How did she explain? She'd been curious. Worried. "How did it go?"

Ken let out a deep sigh. "I agreed to be his partner and then almost instantly regretted it when the club he brought me to, the one he's basing his business upon, was lit on fire by vengeful thieves."

She felt the blood drain from her face as her hand came up to cover her mouth. What if something had happened to Ace or her brother? She swallowed down a lump as she whispered. "A fire?"

Ken mumbled a curse under his breath and then scrubbed his face. "I shouldn't have told you all of that. I'm too tired."

"Yes, you should have," she said stepping closer, swallowing down her fear. "I'm not a child anymore, Ken."

He shook his head. "I'm aware of that. Men are circling about you like vultures."

That made her smile. A little. "But more than that, I can help you and you can trust me."

"Trust you? With what?"

The words, the right ones, filled her thoughts. "With information. Decisions."

He frowned. "Decisions like allowing a questionable lord to court you."

She crossed her arms. She was done being quiet. Something in her had been shifting and now, suddenly, she didn't want to hold back. "You just spent the night with him. Was he that questionable?"

Ken's shoulders fell. "No. Truth be told, he's smart, brave, and honorable."

Warmth slid down her spine. Was she winning? "He's a good man. Committed to his family."

Ken grimaced. "He's still not good enough for you."

"And who is?" she asked, moving closer with a smile. Calling him out didn't mean she needed to be angry or mean.

Ken let out a heavy breath. "No one."

"Ken." She touched her brother's arm. "You have to let me make some decisions for myself. About what I want. About what will really make me happy. You know I've never cared about society."

He grimaced. "I know."

She rested her head on his shoulder, the scent of smoke filling her nostrils. Her gut roiled again at the thought of a fire. Was her brother all right? He looked fine. Was Ace? "I want to see him tomorrow. Make sure he's all right."

"I don't think—"

"Ken," She bit back. She wasn't taking no for an answer this time.

With a tentative nod, Ken finally mumbled. "All right. You win."

Perhaps he was tired. Or maybe, he'd finally realized she was capable too.

But with a smile she tugged on his arm. "I'll warm some water for you so you can bathe in the kitchen. You can't go to bed smelling like that."

He sniffed at himself. "It was awful, Em. And Ace, he knew exactly what to do."

That warmed her heart. Because she might not always know what to say but she knew her feelings. And they all belonged to Ace.

CHAPTER TWELVE

ACE WOKE the next morning to a knock at his bedroom door.

"Ace?" Anna called, her high voice making him smile despite the exhaustion that pulled at every limb.

"What is it?" he asked, propping on one elbow as he scrubbed his face, trying to clear the sleep fog from his mind.

"A missive arrived for you. From a Baron Boxby. I thought…"

He stripped back the covers, shrugging on a shirt and breeches before he crossed the room to open the door.

His angelic sister stood on the other side, nibbling at her lip. "I'm sorry to wake you."

"It's all right," he said, lightly ruffling her hair. At seventeen, it likely was no longer an appropriate gesture but he supposed he still thought of her as the baby of the family. He took the missive she held, tearing it open.

His mouth parted in surprise at the invitation to walk in the park with the baron and his sister.

What could this meeting be about?

If it was just with Boxby, he'd understand that they'd be discussing business or the events of last night.

Or if Mirabelle had come to ask him to escort her, he'd know the

Emily and Mirabelle were conspiring. But an invitation to see both the Boxbys together…

All the sleep vanished from his mind as he started down to the kitchen to heat the water for a bath.

Three hours later, he found himself at the entrance of Hyde Park.

He caught sight of brother and sister walking toward him, both looking as pensive as he felt.

But the moment his gaze caught Emily's, her face broke out into a large, unguarded smile. And everything in him relaxed.

What was it about this woman that brought him such untamable joy?

He took a half step forward, his heart kicking up in his chest.

Boxby waved. "Good to see you looking so well."

He nodded. They'd returned to the club to tell East all that they'd discovered. The fire had been doused, Edge had been found, and Arabella had seemed fine, a relief to be certain. What was more, the group of owners had all arrived and they'd decided to hand the location of the thieves over to the crown. A group of men that size required the military. "You too."

Boxby nodded and the three of them began to walk. To Ace's surprise, Boxby fell behind, allowing Ace to escort Emily. "You're sure you're all right?" she asked, her hand slipping into the crook of his arm.

He looked at her profile, the air stalling in his throat as he cleared it. "I'm fine."

She nodded. "That's good. I just needed to see you for myself after last night."

Had she been worried? What had Boxby told her?

What would it be like to have a woman worry after him like this all the time? That was one of the traits that was so tempting about this woman. After a life of caring for everyone else, she soothed him. "Emily," he whispered her name. "I'm fine. Better. Thanks to you, I've been able to fund the club and provide for my—"

"Oh but," she started, biting her lip. "Wasn't your other club attacked? Is it safe?"

He smiled a bit despite himself. "It's safe enough. Many businesses have their dangers."

"But you could be hurt!"

He wished to wrap his arm about her, wrap her up against his side. "It's an unfortunate drawback of being male, I suppose. But the choice has already been made. I can't afford to change it and I need to see it through in order to see my family's finances secured." Besides, he'd never been the sort of man to let a bit of danger scare him away from anything.

She glanced back at her brother before her gaze returned to Ace. "I could help you. I have an inheritance. With it—"

He gave his head a quick jerk as a fresh wave of irritation washed over him. He hated that she'd even offered.

While he'd loved her help, it was his job to take care of her, or at least he wanted it to be, not the other way around. "Emily, not only would I never take you from your brother, if I ever could marry you, I'd provide for you." Ace glanced back at the baron, who still trailed behind him. As a man who'd do anything to protect his sisters, he could never steal another man's sister away.

She fell silent but she nodded her understanding but her eyes looked sad.

"You do understand, don't you?"

"I do," she cast her gaze to the ground. "It's part of what I find so wonderful about you."

He stopped, looking down to smile at her but a cluster of people caught his notice. The park was quiet and the group of men stood off to the side, staring directly at Ace and Emily. And their clothes…

He scrunched his brows as one of them raised a pistol.

He only had a moment to react but he jerked Emily against his front, twisting to shield her as the noise of the shot and the lead ball whizzed past him at the same moment.

A burning sting ripped through his arm and he ducked his head to cover Emily more.

"Ace," Boxby yelled from just behind.

Ace didn't need to hear more and without a thought, he dropped them both to the ground, covering Emily with his body.

The smell of burning hair filled his nostrils. Somehow, the second ball had singed his hat, knocking it from his head and burning his hair.

Emily screamed under him, burrowing deep into his chest as he wrapped her in his arms.

He needed to get her out of here, bring her to safety.

Boxby fired a return shot, scattering the men long enough for Ace to roll forward and pull out his own weapon. "Get behind me!" he yelled to Emily. He didn't have long to pack the powder and fill it with lead, but he needed to be ready to return fire.

The third man fired, but the ball flew wide. With a roar he rose and started after them, drawing out his short sword.

But they'd already dispersed and he skidded to a stop, not wanting to leave Emily. He looked back, her frightened eyes staring at his right side. The color had drained from her face. "Ace?"

He looked down to see blood pouring down his arm. Damn. He'd been shot.

———

EMILY COULDN'T QUITE process all that had just happened.

Ace had saved her life.

And he'd been hurt as a consequence.

She rose, her knees knocking together as she stood, moving toward him. "Ace?" she repeated uselessly, her trembling hands reaching for him. "You're bleeding."

"I'll be all right." And then he pulled her against his front, moving them both toward the bushes. "Let's move to the cover of the trees."

"I'm fine," she answered, the shaking of her voice belying her words. "It's you who is injured."

He glanced down at his arm. "It's only a flesh wound. I can already tell."

Boxby came next to them, pushing them both toward the trees.

"Normally, I'd send you to fetch the carriage, but with the injury, I think it best you stay put with Emily while I find one of our vehicles."

Ace nodded. "I'll not argue that."

She squeezed his other arm, fear still pumping through her as he wrapped an arm about her and shuttled her off toward the cover of the trees.

"What was that?" she asked the moment they'd reached a cluster of plants and were hidden from view.

He didn't answer, his gaze scanning the park about them.

"Did it...did it have to do with last night?"

"Likely, it did." He pulled her even closer, his eyes closing for a moment. "I've brought trouble to your door."

She shook her head. She could see why he'd say that. He had asked her brother to join his club. But he was not responsible for the criminals that had just attacked them. "That's not true."

"Emily." He drew in a ragged breath then pulled back to look down into her eyes. "I'm a criminal. I've lied, I've falsified documents. I've spied on my own brother for my gain. And that trouble will find you. It already has."

Pain radiated through her at his words. But then she straightened. "You have been protecting and providing for your family under harrowing circumstances. I refuse to see you for anything other than what you are. A provider. A brave, kind man." Then she touched his cheek. "You just saved my life, Ace. Tell me I'm not safer by your side."

Pain clouded his features as slid a hand down her back. "I've already told you. My future is nothing but grim."

She'd share her heart and for once, she'd not apologize for it. "And what will mine be like without you?" She stared up at him, needing him to understand. "I'll never feel for anyone else the way I do you."

For a moment he just stared at her and then he began to lower his head as though he would kiss her.

Her breath caught.

"Ace," Ken called from the other side of the trees. "I've got the carriage."

Ace's head snapped up as he, still holding her close, began moving them both toward the vehicle.

"What happens next?" she asked, wrapping an arm about his waist.

"We get you to safety."

She nodded, but what she really wished to know was what happened next between them.

CHAPTER THIRTEEN

THE MOMENT they entered the carriage, Ken took Emily's arm, sitting on the forward-facing bench with her.

Ace didn't blame him. If it had been Mirabelle or Anna…

But he wanted Emily tucked against his side still.

He worked his injured arm. Despite the blood, it was a minor wound. He'd clean it as soon as he arrived home.

It hurt like hell, but he ignored the pain, thinking instead about Emily.

She'd nearly been shot today. And her words about only being happy with him had stoked the fire burning inside him and he didn't know if he could put that flame out.

He had to try.

He'd been telling her the truth about not having a future to offer.

Still. Looking at her now, pale and afraid, he wished to pull her close, protect her in the circle of his arms.

He wished to hold her close, keep her there.

"Why are they attacking us in the park?" Boxby bit out.

Ace shook his head. "I don't know." This could be an extension of burning the club, the thieves' revenge plot. Or, the military might have attacked and now they were on the run and looking to retaliate?

"As soon as you're safely home, I'll see East and find out. We'll get to the bottom of this. I guarantee it will all be sorted soon."

Boxby grimaced. "And what of your family?"

Ace's stomach dropped. If they'd known he was in the park, did the attackers know where his home was? Had they attempted to hurt his brothers and sisters? His fist clenched, causing his wound to give a painful throb.

"We have to go there now." Emily tapped her brother's arm.

Boxby shook his head. "We should get you home safely first."

Emily lifted her hand in denial, her chin snapping up. "Mirabelle might need us. We need to go now."

Ace wasn't sure why, but Boxby gave a tentative nod. "Fine."

Ace rapped up on carriage wall, shouting out the address. The carriage veered to the left. Tension knotted inside him as they made their way through London, leaving the posh east end toward Cheapside.

They finally arrived and relief rushed through Ace to see the house looking normal, the slightly faded red door, unharmed.

He burst from the carriage and bolted up the stairs, throwing open the front door to find a startled Rush standing in the middle of the entry. "What the bloody—" He clamped his mouth shut, his gaze travelling over Ace's shoulder.

Ace glanced behind him, to see Emily and Boxby enter the house.

The air rushed from his lungs. Now that he knew all was well here, he realized that Emily was seeing his home. It was nothing like her posh townhouse.

Would she begin to understand their real differences being here?

"Is Mirabelle here?" she asked. "Is everything all right?"

"What is she talking about, Ace?" Rush asked.

"Acton?" Anna called, appearing at the top of the stairs. "What's wrong? Are you bleeding?"

Acton. His given name. Even his family rarely used his full first name.

But the question sparked the swarming of all his siblings.

Mirabelle was next, racing down the stairs toward him.

Then came Triston, Gris, and Fulton all of them with brown hair and piercing dark eyes. Rush filing in last, his dark eyes piercing into Ace's as he stood up straighter, pushing to the front.

And everyone was talking.

The babble of questions so loud, no one person could be heard.

He was used to it all.

Really.

"We need to attend your wound," Emily's voice called over the din, quieting everyone as she threaded her arm through her brother's.

"My arm is fine," he said, despite the pain. It was the least of his concerns at the moment. "I'm more concerned about what might happen next."

"Precisely. That's why we should take your sisters and leave London. Now. Are you capable of the journey?" Emily's jaw was set at a jaunty, commanding angle that he'd never seen before.

The room went dead silent in a second as everyone turned to her.

"Yes. I'll be fine."

"What did you just say?" Rush asked Emily before turning to him. "What happened to your arm?"

"Who is this?" Triston demanded, his arms crossing over his massive chest.

"Leave London?" Anna gasped. "For how long?"

Mirabelle came to Emily's side, a soft smile on her lips. "What have you done with my shy friend?"

Emily laughed, a light sound that filled Ace with a bit of hope.

Boxby met his eye, giving a slight nod of affirmation.

Looking at his brothers Ace made a decision. "I've got a few minutes to tell you everything and then Miss Boxby is right. I'm going to take the girls away from London. Both the Den of Sins and Hell's Corner will need your help."

He watched his brothers react, Gris pulling up straighter, his chest puffing out and Rush rumbled, his fists clenching at his sides.

Gris, always the lady's man, winked at Emily, while Triston punched Gris in the arm, saving Ace the trouble.

Of course, Gris didn't know Ace hadn't shared his feelings for

Emily with anyone, but if Gris winked like that again, he'd be facing his eldest brother's wrath.

Boxby stepped closer to Ace. "I'll stay with the women. You explain to your brothers."

Ace nodded. "I'll have to write to East as well. He needs to know." And then he looked at Rush. "You'll have to deliver the message."

"To him?" Rush asked his lip curling.

But Ace shook his head. "And you'll have to be civil. He may now stand between us and the devil that nips at our heels."

Rush's teeth clenched together. "Explain."

Ushering his brothers into the living room, he quickly detailed the events of last night and how East had given him the paperwork and partnership to secure the future of their club.

"You're jesting," Gris growled out. "He, of all people, helped us?"

Ace debated telling them about East's request to meet his sisters. "Tell him we're going to travel with Boxby but that we'll be back in London as soon as I know it's safe. What's more, tell him that you'll divide your numbers to protect both clubs."

"Why are we protecting our competition?" Rush asked, shifting to lean casually against the wall. It was an act. His brother was anything but casual.

"Because..." Ace understood their frustration. Not only did they know that East had the power to destroy Ace but they also had their own reservations about the earl. "He's our partner now and we might need his favors in the future."

"Fuck." Gris pushed out through his clenched teeth as Tris punched the palm of his own hand.

They were each hard and strong in their own way and Ace knew this was difficult for them. But there wasn't a choice here. They could not work against him and undo all that he'd accomplished. "Tell me you understand."

None of his brothers looked happy with his words but they each nodded, acknowledging that they'd do as he wished.

Pivoting to the desk, he scrolled a hasty note to East and then started out of the room again, turning just before he reached the door. "Take care of yourselves."

Rush gave a quick jerk of his chin in acknowledgment. "Take care of our sisters."

Gris craned his neck. "And the pretty brunette. Miss Boxby, was it?"

Ace took one step back toward his brother, his finger lifting. "Not now, Gris."

But Gris only smiled, his trouble grin, the one he gave when he intentionally stirred the pot.

Ace ignored the look and pivoted to return to the entry.

It was time to save the women he cared most about. All of them.

———

EMILY LOOKED across the carriage for the hundredth time in less than an hour as they rumbled down the road, out of London toward their estate in Amesbury. Ace sat across from her, his gaze unwavering.

Next to her, Mirabelle chatted amicably while on her other side, Anna sat silently, her head dipped and her hands folded.

But she didn't have the ability to wonder about the young woman with Ace's eyes so fixed on her.

Heat filled her cheeks as she realized they'd be in the same house for…how long? Days? Weeks?

And would her brother allow him to court her?

Ken had been more receptive. Allowing the outing in the park. Taking Ace and his sisters out of London.

They'd left Ace's carriage for his brothers to use while they'd all climbed into Ken's vehicle. It was a bit tight but they'd stay at an inn tonight, finishing the journey tomorrow. But the lack of space wasn't what had her the most uncomfortable.

By far, Ace's unwavering gaze is what had her shifting in her seat yet again as her eyes skittered from his once again.

Emily nearly breathed a sigh of relief when they finally reached the inn, had a simple stew, and retired to begin travel early the next morning.

She climbed the stairs, exhausted but well aware that she'd hardly sleep knowing that Ace was just a few doors away.

She turned to find him just behind her, Mirabelle on his arm.

Her brother showed her to her room and she watched as Ace did the same for his sisters, who'd be sharing a room.

Since the events in the park this afternoon, she'd not even had a chance to say thank you nor had anyone tended his arm.

The moment she reached her room, she rang for a maid and gathered up the supplies she'd need for first aid because his wound still hadn't been wrapped in anything to stem the flow of blood.

As quietly as she could, she slipped from her room and made her way down the hall to knock on Ace's door.

"Who is it?" he called, sounding muffled.

"It's me," she whispered back, knowing full well she could not be discovered in the hallway.

There was silence for a moment before the door opened a crack.

"Emily?" he whispered, but she didn't respond as she understood his hesitation in responding. He'd already removed his blood-stained shirt.

"May I..." she started, swallowing as she cleared her throat. Then she held up the supplies. "I came to tend you."

He opened the door and pulled her inside, closing it quickly behind her. "You shouldn't be here."

"I know. I was just worried and I wanted to say thank you—" But her words were cut off as his mouth descended over hers. And then she forgot all the words as his kiss stole the air from her lungs and the words from her lips.

She wrapped her arms about his bare neck, the feel of his skin under her hands so much more than she'd ever dreamed. Her fingers danced over the muscles, tracing the ridges as his mouth devoured hers.

Her fingertips slipped down his arms until, suddenly, he shuddered.

She gasped, realizing she'd touched his wound. "Oh! I'm so sorry."

He smiled down at her. "It's fine."

She looked down his arm, seeing the angry red slash across his biceps. "Let me help you."

With a nod, he crossed to take a seat as she uncorked the brandy. He hissed as she poured the amber liquid over the wound. Despite his many assertions that he was fine, she realized that his face was paler than normal, his features drawn. Gently, she wrapped the arm in clean linen and then secured the end.

Without thought, she brushed his hair back from his forehead. "You should rest."

He gave a quick nod. "Would you mind leaving the brandy? Might help me sleep."

"Of course." She turned to go but his hand came to her hip. He pulled her close, his head coming to rest on her chest just above her bosom.

As he let out a long breath, she wrapped her arms about his neck, pressing her cheek to the top of his head. "Thank you for saving my life today. I—" So many words crowded her mouth. How much she cared. How no man had ever been as brave or strong as him.

But he gave his head the smallest shake. "This is thanks enough."

And then he settled her closer.

CHAPTER FOURTEEN

THE NIGHT HAD BEEN long and painful, the day in the carriage equally so, but as the carriage pulled up in front of the Boxby's estate, Ace felt as though he might be at his lowest point.

His father had owned a home like this, he knew that. But Ace had never visited.

This estate was massive, only growing larger the closer they got, the tree-lined drive perfectly and elegantly manicured to complement the stone-and-brick façade. Emily belonged in a place like this, not in his shabby townhome in Cheapside.

His arm and his head throbbed.

Pulling up to the stately double door, enormous granite steps in front, their party was met by a small army of servants who whisked them inside and up to stately rooms.

A bath and a large tray of food awaited Ace in his room and he stripped immediately, hoping that a long soak might cure some of what ailed him.

He ought to be happy. His sisters were safe and once the thieves were disbanded, he'd have what he'd been seeking.

He'd gotten everything he'd wanted prior to meeting Emily.

But somewhere along the way, his heart had begun to yearn for more. Yearn for her.

He sank deeper into the water, his arms resting on the sides of the tub. Even this bath was a reminder of all the reasons he couldn't have her. Did each person who'd arrive have a hot tub of water like this? How many servants had it taken to accommodate five simultaneous baths ready precisely for their arrival?

He rose, drying himself off, gingerly shrugging on the waiting dressing gown and eating a few bites of food before retiring to the bed. He was tired and weak, the effort of appearing normal having sapped all his energy.

He closed his eyes, tossing an arm over his eyes as his other biceps throbbed in pain.

Shivering a bit after the bath, he heaved himself off the bed long enough to crawl under the covers. A knock sounded at the door. Was it Emily? Had she come to check on him.

"Ace?" Boxby's voice called. "How are you feeling?"

"Fine," he lied. "Is everything all right with the women?"

The door cracked open and Boxby peaked his head in the room. "They're fine. You look like death."

He lifted his head, moving his arm up for a moment. "You're not that lucky."

Boxby grinned. "Lucky? We just became partners. Why would I want you to expire now?"

Ace didn't bother to mention that he was making Boxby's plans for Emily much more difficult. Even he knew that. Imagine if Mirabelle or Anna fell in love with someone so wildly inappropriate. How would he react to such a situation? Boxby had been damned gracious.

"I don't think my health is as bad as all that." He'd just looked at the wound. While rough, it didn't appear infected. At least not yet. "But if it is—"

Boxby stepped further into the room. "I owe you a debt of gratitude for the way you saved Emily yesterday. Know that if anything does happen to you, I'll see your family is cared for."

Ace gave a quick nod, grateful for the baron's words. He was beyond grateful. Relief made him sink further into the bed as emotion clogged his throat. "Thank you."

To know that his sister would be tended by someone like Boxby lightened the load on his shoulders tremendously. Ace had picked a good man to be his first partner. He closed his eyes. "I think I'll see if some sleep won't help me to live and you not to increase your dependents."

Boxby gave a little chuckle. "Fair enough. I'll let you rest."

Ace closed his eyes. He liked to ask the baron, beg really, to trade that favor for a different purpose. To be allowed the chance to court Emily...

Still, he'd always had his priorities. And no matter how much he wished the circumstances were different, he wasn't at liberty to court a woman like Emily and his responsibilities had always been crystal clear.

But he fell asleep dreaming of rich brown hair and warm eyes. Emily's voice whispered through his mind as her soft arms held him as he slept.

———

EMILY HADN'T SEEN Ace in two days. She was growing concerned.

She'd asked her brother to check on him twice.

Ken had dutifully gone to Ace's room and come back reporting that the man was *fine*.

When she'd asked what he meant by fine, Ken had given her an incredulous look. "Fine is fine."

She'd attempted not to huff an annoyed breath but failed. "Fine gives me absolutely no information."

Ken's brows had drawn together. "Why have you become so surly? It's exactly the information you asked for."

She lifted her hands to either side as she punctuated the air. "Surly? I'm not surly, I'm just no longer complacent. And why you can't understand that I'd like more information about the health of a man who suffered a wound while saving my life, I'll never know. But rest assured, I do need more. I'm worried about him."

Ken had given her an odd look, before he'd let out a long sigh. "I'll ask again. But perhaps you might understand that he only wishes to share so much with me. Men don't go about just talking about their feelings with each other, you know."

Emily shook her head. She did know.

Which was why there was little to do but go ask herself. And not in a visit that was watched. Ace would be unlikely to share anything with Ken or servants in attendance.

She waited until the house had quieted and then wrapping her dressing gown tightly around her middle, she'd set out without even a candle. Best not to announce her nightly activities.

She'd crept up the flight of stairs to Ace's room, knowing the one in which he'd been placed.

Standing outside the door, she drew in a fortifying breath before she raised her hand and softly knocked.

He didn't call out and she shifted, wondering if he was there. Was Ace sleeping?

But a moment later, the door opened and he appeared, quickly pulling her inside before he closed the door again.

Emily didn't have a moment to even ask a question before his lips had descended over hers, their bodies pressed together in the most satisfying way as her back thumped against the closed door.

She wrapped her hands about his neck, her fingers playing over his skin as their tongues danced together. Minutes passed before they broke apart long enough for her to ask. "You're all right, then?"

"Fine," he murmured before he captured her lips again. Why did the word on his lips have so much more meaning?

Perhaps because she could feel just how well he was doing. His arms were as strong as ever. His lips confident and in command, his body muscular and hard against her soft curves. "I've been so worried."

"About me?" He smiled before he gave her another, softer brush of lips. "Emily, what have I done to deserve such tenderness?"

She blinked in surprise. What had he done? But before she began the list, he kissed her again, his tongue sliding along the seam of her lips. She sighed into his mouth, so glad to be with him again. "I've missed you," she murmured against him.

He lifted away a bit. "I've missed you too."

"Your wound is healing? No fever?"

"None."

"You'll be all right?"

"Fine."

She laughed a little at the word and likely because relief made her limbs limp. "Oh, thank goodness."

He swiped a thumb over her cheek. "And you? Have you recovered from your scare?"

She stared up at him. "I'm fine." She shook her head. Why did he even need to ask? "I'm not the one who was shot."

He gave her a small, one-sided smile, the sort that made her stomach flip in the strangest way. "It's only a graze, love."

That word, love, on his lips made her stomach flip again, her heart hammering in her chest as she looked up at him. "Ace."

He lowered his head, slowly, deliberately, his lips melding to hers as his hands slid to her jaw, cupping her face between them as he tasted her over and over. "I'm sorry I worried you."

"Don't apologize," she breathed, her voice catching part way through.

He shook his head. "I wish..." But then he lowered his mouth again, the kiss lingering, growing, deepening until Emily had lost all sense of time and place. Only Ace mattered, only the feel of his body against hers.

Which was why she'd hardly noticed when he lifted her up, wrapping an arm under her behind as he carried her. It wasn't until he went to lay her on the bed, the soft mattress under her back, that she realized what she'd allowed.

And despite the depth of her desire, she froze, stiffening. She should not be on his bed. "Ace," she said again, but this time his name came as a sigh tinged with her concern.

He stilled too, looking down at her. "Emily, don't be afraid." His thumb brushed along her cheek. "Whenever you wish to stop, just say the word. I would never..." He drew in a ragged breath. "You've given me so much these last days, I wanted to give a bit of pleasure back to you but not if it will upset you."

The tension eased a bit. "It didn't upset me..." She licked her lips and his eyes darted to her mouth again. Heat settled low in her stomach. "I just..." She searched for the words to explain. "There is no formal promise between us despite the affection I think we both share."

"We do."

"And while I know I'll never feel about anyone else the way I feel about you, I would be remiss if I..." She stopped again. She trusted him with her life and with her feelings. But he'd been clear about not wishing to marry, and she could not give herself to him knowing that.

He brushed a stray lock of hair back from her forehead. "Emily," he said, then dipped down, kissing the hollow of her neck. "I want to touch you, feel your pleasure, but I'll not take your maidenhead. I swear you'll still be a virgin when I am done."

She swallowed, excitement sizzling like butter on a hot pan. But there was something in the words that cooled her ardor too. If he were protecting her virginity did that mean he'd never consider a future with her?

But she forgot to ask as his lips started to slide lower along the neckline of her dressing gown.

Her nipples tightened as the dressing gown loosened, her night rail beneath having a wide neckline that allowed him access to much of her chest.

"Emily," he said, his breath warm against her skin. "Do you wish for me to stop?"

She shook her head. "Kiss me more."

He did, his lips sliding over the soft cotton and lace of her night rail until he reached the peak of her breast and sucked it into his mouth through the fabric.

She cried out, the pleasure almost more than she could bear as his hand came to the other breast, massaging the flesh in his palm.

He'd settled between her legs and as she squirmed in pleasure, she found the place between her legs that ached with need the most was rewarded by the movement. She moaned, wanting more.

He obliged, seeming to understand exactly what she craved as his hand found the hem of her night rail and slid the thin material up her thigh.

When his fingers brushed the curls nestled at her apex, his mouth still working her nipple, the throb of pleasure was so intense, she squeezed her fingertips into his neck, needing an anchor from the pleasure.

But she soon realized that it was only the beginning.

As he started a rhythm, lightly massaging her most intimate places with the pad of his finger, pleasure grew and until she was mad from it.

This was why she'd pushed so hard to take what she wanted, why she'd stop hiding behind fear.

Because with chances came great reward.

And risk.

But who could think about that now? And as the pleasure reached dizzying heights, the kind that stole all reason, she forgot to think, just feeling until she fell over the edge of her pleasure.

Ace slowed his touches and kisses as she spasmed with the force of her finish. And when she'd floated down, he wrapped his arms tighter about her, holding her close all the while whispering words of comfort in her ear.

She didn't hear them, more felt them as she slid her hands down his back, drifting off to sleep in his arms.

CHAPTER FIFTEEN

ACE HELD Emily even as she slept, her long dark lashes resting on her cheeks.

Watching her come undone had been beautiful.

He'd like to watch her like that a thousand more times at least.

But it had been selfish on his part to even ask for the once. He had no future to give, only a few scraps of pleasure in the present.

Waiting until she was deep in sleep, he slid from the bed, wrapping a blanket about her to keep her warm. Then lifting her from the mattress, he began carrying her from the room.

She woke instantly. "Your arm," she cried, half sitting up.

He smiled, despite himself. "Always worrying after me." How he loved that, craved this gentle affection she so effortlessly gave him.

She wiggled and he set her down. She was right, at least in part. His arm was still sore and not as strong as usual. He could hold her, but not with her moving like that.

She stared up at him. "Why don't we lie back down? We could sleep or I could..." Even in the dark, heat filled her cheeks and he knew she meant she'd like to return some pleasure to him.

The idea of it made his still rock-hard staff throb as it ached for relief.

But he'd not take it. Not now. The only reason he'd been able to justify what he'd just done to himself was because it had been for her.

"You need your rest and so do I," he lied, stroking her cheek. But guilt shuddered through him as her features instantly fell.

"Oh dear, I've overtaxed you." There she went. Worrying about him again.

He kissed her temple and then the other. "Not at all but it's best we return you to your room before your absence is discovered."

She gave a tentative nod. "All right."

Placing a hand at her back, he started to guide her toward the door when she stopped, looking over at him, her bottom lip caught between her teeth. "You protected my virginity, yes?"

"Of course," he soothed, his hand spreading out on her back.

But she didn't look relieved, rather, her brows drew deeper together. "Because you still have no intention of pursuing me, do you?"

He stopped, looking down at her, pain pulsing through him. "It's not a matter of intent."

"What is it then?"

He tried to pull her closer but she resisted. "I'm not in a position to wed you, Emily."

"But things are different now. You've secured your family's future."

"I've already explained. I've secured their future but not my own. And there is no way to do so. I'm a liar and I cannot contain the lie forever. It's not possible."

Pain pulled at her eyes and mouth as a tear collected on her lashes. "But I already told you, I'll take whatever time you can give me. I don't want anyone else."

He shook his head. "I could never live with myself if I did that to you. If I abandon you because of my own deceptions."

Her trembling lips pressed together. "I've made a promise to myself that I'll speak my mind and so I'll say what I feel now. You ought to have just taken my maidenhead. I'll never give it to another."

That made him ache. He wanted it, wanted her with a passion he could hardly deny. He was in love with this woman. "You feel that way now."

She shook her head. "I know who I am. No one trusts me to understand myself, but I do. You are the only one for me, of that I am certain."

And then she tightened the belt of her dressing gown and started for the door. Just as she reached it, she turned back to him. "You have to choose me, you know, the way I've chosen you."

That cut deep. Far worse than the wound on his arm. "I have chosen you, Emily. Don't you understand that? You think I'll marry someone else? I won't. I've chosen to put your life and your needs over my own desires. I'd give anything...anything to be with you. But I won't hurt you that way. Not ever."

He heard her rush of breath, her hand covering her mouth.

He stepped up to her, reaching down to pull her in his arms again, and then quietly, he slipped open the door and carried her up to her room.

After she entered her room, closing the door and locking it behind her, he let out a long exhale of regret.

He wasn't sure which part of the evening he should have done differently but he knew he'd erred.

Rubbing his temples, he started back for his room. Stopping, he looked back at the door. Should he knock and attempt to explain more?

Explain what?

He'd spoken the truth.

With another deep sigh of regret, he returned to his bed chamber.

———

EMILY STARED OUT THE WINDOW, the bright and sunny day mocking her tired eyes. After she'd left Ace, she'd hardly slept a wink.

Because his words had settled somewhere deep inside. There was the rejection of course. But underneath that hurt, she believed him.

She'd always believed him. Believed that he was a good man

despite the lies, believed that he understood her like no one else. Believed that he told her the truth, he was choosing not to give her a future with him for her own benefit.

Was she a fool? Perhaps. But for the first time in her life, her foolishness was hers to own and suffer the consequences of alone.

And deep in her heart, she believed that he shared her feelings and wanted what was best for her.

But she also knew he cared deeply for his siblings, which meant they couldn't just run away together. She'd not leave Ken, and Ace would never leave his family either.

Which made the situation near hopeless.

Tears pricked at her eyes but she blinked them away, determined not to indulge in the emotion that had plagued her all morning.

She sat in the library, a book in her lap that she'd yet to even open as she looked out over the grounds.

She'd always loved this place, felt at peace here in ways she never did in the city. But not today.

"Don't you look dreadful!" Mirabelle called from the doorway as she rushed into the room, her sister Anna just behind her.

Anna, exceptionally quiet, was near angelic in her appearance with large blue eyes and lush blonde hair. She looked far more like a renaissance painting than an actual person.

"Do I?" she asked with a sigh. "I feel fairly awful too."

Mirabelle grimaced. "You and Ace. I finally saw him today and while he's up and moving, he's as grumpy as I've ever seen him."

"He was shot," Anna said, raising a single finger.

"He didn't look bothered by that," Mirabelle said, her hands coming to her hips. But then they dropped again as she slid into the seat across from Emily. "But you don't need to hear all this. I'm sorry. I already asked for your aid and you gave it. I just thought that he'd be happier once he got what he wanted."

"Happier?" Emily asked as she leaned forward, her attention on Mirabelle even sharper than it had been before.

"He's not sad, just quiet," Anna replied. "Like me." But her mouth dipped into a frown. "Isn't he?"

Emily looked back and forth between the two sisters. Ace was always so strong and capable but was he hurting? He'd had so much responsibility. And such a heavy burden to bear.

Mirabelle shook her head. "I'm not so certain. I know he's the one who was given the title thanks to our father, but it's come with so much worry. Of providing. And then there's the risk of being caught."

"He talks about that a great deal. The fact that he has no future. And he won't marry because of it."

Mirabelle made a small cry of dissent, the color draining from Anna's face. Anna's voice whispered, "But he's secured the club."

"That provides for us," Mirabelle replied. "And our brothers. But it does little to protect him."

Emily winced. That was the truth.

Anna clapped her hand to her mouth, tenting over her face. "You have to help him."

Emily blinked in surprise. What could she do?

But even as she thought the words, she knew. She'd thought it already. They could leave...go to Paris or Florence or... "The only way that I could help him would mean he'd have to leave England. For good."

The two sisters looked at one another. Mirabelle closed her eyes. "And what are the alternatives? If he stays here, we get to keep him, but he could be caught."

"He might not," Emily said, hoping to be helpful.

"But then you said he won't wed because of the threat of being discovered." Anna pressed a hand to her stomach. "Has he really given up his entire future for ours?"

Emily's heart ached for them. For Ace too. And for herself.

Silence fell over the women and seconds turned into minutes, each lost in their own thoughts. "You have to do it," Anna finally said. "You have to marry him and take him away."

Mirabelle shook her head. "That would mean Emily would have to leave her family too."

"Oh. Right," Anna said, wincing. "Sorry. Clearly, I need to work on thinking these things through. I've never had to before."

Emily smiled. "It's all right. You're doing your best."

"You're always so kind, Emily." Mirabelle rose, taking her friend's hand in hers.

Anna rose too, coming to her other side. "I didn't mean to overstep. I never seem to say the right thing…"

Emily's heart lurched in her chest and she rose, grasping Anna in her arms. She knew that exact feeling and her heart went out to the young woman. "Speak your heart, Anna. You'll learn more about it that way." As she stepped back again, she took a deep breath. She loved Ken very much, but Ken would marry, start a family of his own.

This decision was about her future and she knew precisely what she needed to do.

CHAPTER SIXTEEN

ONE OF THE advantages of being in the country on an estate was the amount of land at his disposal to ride.

He'd been out on one of Boxby's geldings all morning, attempting to work out the frustration that had settled deep in his bones.

The picturesque landscape of rolling hills dotted with trees, leaves turned to vibrant reds, oranges, and yellows, had done little to quell his mounting frustration. And no amount of exercise seemed to do the trick either.

Holding Emily close, feeling her come apart in his arms had only made him want her more.

He handed over the horse to the groom and then made his way inside, intent upon a bath and then...

He didn't know. Wallowing? Possibly. Daydreaming? Most certainly. He was normally a man of action but much as he tried to think of a solution, he just couldn't find one to his problem with Emily.

How did he make her his forever? It simply wasn't possible.

With a growl of frustration, he strode into the kitchen and started for the back stairs when the butler came out of the butler's pantry, snapping to attention at the sight of Ace. "Lord Smith," the man called, giving a short bow. "A letter has arrived for you."

A letter? Was it from one of his brothers? His stomach tightened with worry. Had something happened at one of the clubs?

The butler held out a tray, Ace instantly recognizing the seal as the Earl of Easton's. East. Had East and the other lords that ran the Den of Sins cleared the city of the thieves already?

Taking the stairs two at a time, he hurried to his room, closing the door behind him as he broke open the seal with the letter opener.

The first line stopped his breath.

The Marquess of Devonhall, the man he claimed to be the heir of, had died.

This was it.

His end had finally come. Ace looked to the ceiling saying a silent prayer of thanks that he'd funded the club and that he had not married Emily. He could be content in prison knowing that the people he loved most all had a future.

And from his cell, he'd not have to witness Emily marry another.

He pulled out the desk chair and sat, prepared to face whatever East said next.

But as he continued scanning down the letter, his eyes widened in surprise, his heart pounding in his ears.

It is with the highest regard that I'd like to inform you that I have every intention of supporting your claim to the marquessate. You have proven yourself a man of honor and integrity and with my support, the man who would receive the title in your place, I'm certain any rumors or doubt will be silenced.

HE DROPPED THE LETTER, blinking several times to try and clear his mind. Had he read that right? Did he actually understand? East's support of his claim would stop any potential investigation from the king. Ace was certain of that. East was the man who would benefit the most if Ace's claim was questioned, so his support meant everything.

He picked up the missive again, his hand shaking, certain that he'd read it wrong only to have his first impression confirmed.

His gaze blurred as he rubbed a hand down his face. East was publicly supporting him.

He'd never imagined...

Never even considered that the earl would give up the title of marquess for his illegitimate brother. It was too much to ask. Too much to hope for.

But here it was.

As a marquess, anything was possible. His sisters were about to become ladies. His brothers lords, and Emily...

Emily was going to be his.

He rose again, determined to share the news with Boxby and ask permission to court Emily. Seek out her hand.

He'd made it two steps toward the door when a knock halted his steps.

Crossing the room, he pulled it open to find Emily on the other side.

He couldn't hide his grin. "What are you doing here?" Had she known? Sensed the change?

But she didn't return his smile as she pushed him back into the room, following him in and closing the door. "I need to speak with you."

"About?" His smile slipped as he reached for her waist, drawing her close. Was something wrong? He'd never allow anything to hurt her.

"Listen to me," she started her hands coming to his biceps. "I know that you claimed you'd never allow me to support you."

"I did." He drew his brows together as he stared down at her, his hands spreading out on the small of her back.

"But." She pressed a hand against her chest, her fingers spreading wide. "I've thought about it and I think we should run away together."

He nearly choked on his own saliva. "Run away?"

"I know you don't want to leave your family but they're settled now and besides, wouldn't you be a greater asset to them in Paris than in prison?"

There was logic there. If prison were still a possibility. "And we'd fund this lifelong trip to Paris with..."

Color rose in her cheeks. "I have more than enough money."

He shook his head. Was she suggesting that she'd leave Ken, her entire life, for him? It stole his breath the lengths this woman would go to help him. He pulled her closer still, until not a breath of air separated them.

"I see you shaking your head. Don't say no. Not yet." Her other hand splayed out on his chest. "Ken will marry. Start a family. He'll be all right without me. I—"

"Emily," he cut her off a second before he captured her lips with his own. By God, he loved this woman.

The kiss lingered and built until they were both breathless, their tongues tangled together.

When he finally lifted his head, she had the dazed look of a woman befuddled by lust, which suited him quite well. He smiled down at her again, lowering his mouth to kiss again and again.

Forever.

But her hands pushed against his chest, her eyes clearing a bit.

"Ace."

"Yes?"

"I..." She swallowed, her expression growing almost pained. "Please don't dismiss my offer. I love you. I want to be with you. Now and always."

Those words melted his heart. That wasn't true, his heart had already been thoroughly defrosted. But it warmed him, a rosy glow filling every fiber of his being. "I love you too. More than I could ever tell you."

He saw the hope spark in her eyes.

"But we're not moving to Paris."

He saw her face fall and he realized he needed to share a great deal more. He'd not hurt her now or ever. But her shoulders squared. "Rome then?"

That made him laugh, his head tossing back. When he looked down again, her eyes were narrowed in question. "How about the north of England, at least for part of the year?"

"The north…" She shook her head and he left her arms to return to his desk and hand her the letter he'd received from East.

She read it and he knew the moment she reached his favorite part. Her hands began to tremble.

He drew her closer as her gaze found his again. "East is going to…" But she couldn't seem to get the words out. Which suited him just fine. He'd much rather kiss her.

And since they were in his room alone…he could think of a few more things he'd like to do as well.

———

WHEN ACE'S lips descended on Emily's again, she knew this kiss wasn't going to end. Not for a long time.

He loved her.

He'd asked her to move to the north of England with him.

Suddenly, she tapped his shoulder. "Wait."

"What?" he asked, lifting his head.

"Does this mean that we're to be married?"

He gave her another glowing smile. "Of course it does. Unless you think Ken will deny me?" He stiffened against her. "I'd not steal a man's sister, Emily, no matter how much I wished to."

She shook her head, joy bubbling inside her. "He'll support the suit of a marquess. I'm sure of it."

Ace lowered his mouth again, kissing her before he whispered against her lips. "In that case, I'm going to thoroughly kiss the woman who is about to become my wife. And when I'm done kissing her lips, I'm moving onto several other areas of her body."

Her breath caught but she didn't respond as he did exactly that. He kissed her mouth, then her cheeks, her forehead, down her neck, his lips sliding along the high collar of her dress.

And when he reached for the row of tiny buttons down her dress, she arched into him, beyond ready to remove some of her clothing.

He made quick work of several articles, making certain to kiss all the skin that became exposed with each layer that was removed.

A few of his items came off as well. His neck cloth, jacket, vest, boots, so that by the time he'd lifted her to carry her to the bed, she was in nothing but her chemise and him in his shirt and breeches.

But it still wasn't enough.

She wanted more of his skin. Pulling on his shirts, Emily managed to get the garment partially up his torso even though he was carrying her, but as he placed her on the bed, he finished the job, pulling the garment over his head.

The sight of his rippling torso made her gasp, and for a moment she just stared. This man was hers.

She sat partially propped on her elbows, her legs dangling over the side of the bed. Emily expected him to cover her body with his but he didn't.

For a moment he just stood there, drinking her in.

And then he reached down, lifting her ankle with a gentle hand until he'd brought it all the way to his lips. He placed a gentle kiss on the inside, the brush of his whiskers adding a slight scratch that only seemed to heighten her pleasure.

But he didn't stop there. He kissed a trail up her calf and over her knee, making her shiver with pleasure as his tongue licked and his teeth nipped at every sensitive spot along the trail of his mouth.

Slowly, he pushed the hem higher until he'd reached her inner thigh.

Her breath came out in short gasps, pleasure pulsing through her with every touch as heat pooled between her legs.

And when his mouth brushed her most sensitive parts, her hips bucked from the bed. Never had she imagined that a touch could bring such pleasure and as he repeated the movement, she found his second pass even better.

But he didn't stop there. On and on he went, kissing her until she could barely stand it, her head thrashing from side to side as she anchored herself by fisting one hand in his hair and the other into the blankets on the bed.

Finally, she broke apart with a cry of pleasure and relief, her body spasming with her finish.

Ace was up in a second, stripping down his breeches and then tugging off her chemise.

She might have been embarrassed but she hardly had a moment as he came down on top of her, their skin rubbing together in the most tantalizing way.

The tip of his manhood pressed against her thick folds but she didn't shy away. Instead, she wrapped her legs about his waist, opening herself up to him as much as possible. This was the man she'd wed. The man who would be hers for the rest of her life. There was nothing left to fear.

CHAPTER SEVENTEEN

PERCHED on the brink of taking Emily's maidenhead, Ace stared down at the woman he loved, her rich brown eyes fixed on his as she silently communicated everything he'd ever secretly wished for.

Her love, her commitment, her desire.

The force of her feelings rocked through him, building a certainty that he'd never been in a more perfect place or time. This was where he belonged.

With whom he belonged. He lowered his mouth, kissing her as he breathed in her scent. Everything about her was made for him.

Slowly, he began to push inside her. He felt her stretch to accommodate him, her body tensing and he stopped again, allowing her time to adjust.

Much as he wanted her, there was no rush. This was only the beginning.

"My love," he whispered against her cheek. "Tell me if we should stop."

"Stop?" she asked, her eyes searching his. "Why would we stop?"

"I don't want to hurt you."

She gave him a small smile. "You would never." And then she kissed him, her muscles relaxing underneath him.

Slowly, he slid into her, her body tight around him, as he seated himself fully inside her.

Never had anything felt so intense like this.

She twined her arms about his neck, her lips locked with his as they kissed, completely joined as one.

And when he slowly pulled out only to push back in, he groaned at the pleasure that pulsed through him.

"Emily," he groaned, burying his face in her neck.

She tightened her arms about his neck. "It's you and me now."

"Always."

He started a slow rhythm, wanting to make sure she was comfortable, but when her hips rose to meet his, he found himself quickening the pace. She matched it, their lips still locked in a kiss as higher and higher they climbed together until he felt her clench around his manhood as a cry fell from her lips.

Her finish sparked his and he pulled out of her, spending his seed onto the blanket underneath them.

"Ace?" She stroked an idle hand down his back. "I likely should have asked this first but..."

"Yes?" He ran his fingers through her hair, as he looked down at her soft features and the light grin that played at her lips.

"When do you wish to wed?"

He laughed a bit. Had she grown concerned? She needn't. He belonged to her, heart and soul. "As soon as your brother will allow."

She smiled at that. "Do you wish to marry here or in London?"

He looked around. Here sounded quite nice to him.

Could his brothers afford to take the time to travel here? He'd want them to attend. "Here, if we can."

"I agree," she sighed and he rolled onto his side, pulling her with him and settling her onto his chest. It was the middle of the afternoon but he heard the sleepiness in her voice. He couldn't blame her.

They'd hardly slept last night and now they'd satisfied their bodies again. "We'll sort it all out after you wake, my love. But either way, we'll be wed before the fall has turned to winter."

She smiled as she traced the muscles of his chest. "That sounds wonderful."

It did. He snuggled her closer, content for the first time in years. He had a future with Emily and that future had never been brighter.

NOTE TO READERS:

Dear Readers,

I promise, I did not leave you in the lurch! Emily and Ace will have their wedding. But before they do, Mirabelle needs to find her happily-ever-after too and she's got her sights set on a certain baron…

Want to find out more? Preorder *A Bet with a Baron* today! And get ready for the entire Smith family to find their happy endings along with a few friends they meet along the way in the "Lords of Scandal" spinoff series, "Lords of Temptation." The Smith brothers are a bit rough around the edges, but we'll see them smoothed out before it's said and done!

All my best,
   Tammy

A BET WITH A BARON

LORDS OF TEMPTATION BOOK ONE

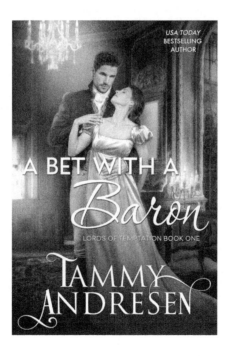

Lady Mirabelle Smith had a secret.

Actually, she had multiple secrets but only the one had dug deep in her thoughts and would not let her alone.

She drew in a breath, her gaze scanning the manicured gardens of the Baron of Boxby's country estate. The lush gardens rustled softly in the summer breeze only enhancing the bucolic air that infused this place.

It was like a fantasy compared with her modest London home.

It was heaven compared with her first home on the east side of London. In retrospect, she had little understanding of how her father had allowed them to live there for so long. But today was not the day for such thoughts. Today was her brother's wedding day.

That same breeze rustled her skirts and an errant lock of her dark brown hair that she attempted to tuck behind her ear. She wished she were blonde like her sister Anna. A true beauty, Anna was often compared to an angel.

No one would mistake Mirabelle for an ethereal figure. Her dark hair and eyes were far more suited to dastardly deeds.

Like keeping secrets. She was a woman used to holding the truth close. As the bastard daughter of the Earl of Easton, she'd grown up understanding the stigma that surrounded her birth. And when her father had orchestrated for her eldest brother to become the heir to a marquessate... the entire family had had to keep that secret.

But that was the sort of falsehood that she'd been able to go days without thinking on, weeks even.

And then she'd had one confidante, her best friend, Emily Boxby. Soon to be Emily Smith. Emily was marrying Mirabelle's eldest brother and officially becoming her sister. Mirabelle couldn't be more thrilled.

And the fact that their legitimate brother, the Earl of Easton, was going to support her brother Ace's claim to the marquessate brought her tantalizingly close to fulfilling her greatest wish, her biggest secret of all.

Mirabelle wished to be a proper lady. Not just in name. Technically, she was Lady Mirabelle. When her brother succeeded to the marquessate, her title as a lady had been solidified. But she didn't just want the name of lady, she wanted to be a lady.

One who was beautiful and gracious, one who was as pretty on the inside as she appeared outwardly.

And most of all, she wanted to be a lady that men of the peerage adored.

Her breath caught in her chest as she moved toward the line of carriages that would take the wedding guests the short distance to the chapel.

Four of her five brothers stood in a line, waiting for her. Four sets of broad shoulders and dark hair standing like centaurs.

Her surly guardians.

Rath came first, the second oldest. His hair was shorn short, his expression ever serious as he watched her move toward them.

Triston was next, his overlong hair, brushing his ears and collars, his expression clearly relaying his feelings about weddings, as surely as if he was muttering the words. "Why would anyone wish to wed?"

Gris was next, his ever ready smile playing at his lips. It wasn't that he was happier than their other brothers. It was more that he caught people off guard with his ease. They were never prepared when he struck.

And there was Fulton. The youngest, he was also the wildest, forever in trouble. Fighting, gaming, and generally spreading mayhem wherever he went.

He was the most heavily muscled of all her brothers, and she knew that he spent a great deal of time boxing, claiming that the exercise kept him out of trouble. She had to shake her head, trying to imagine Fulton even worse than he already was.

Her fifth brother, Ace, was the eldest, the new marquess, and the man who held them all together. Without him, Rush claimed Fulton would be dead in a gutter. Mirabelle wasn't certain about that, but she did know how hard Ace worked for their family. Which is why he deserved to marry a woman as sweet and wonderful as Emily.

Ace was nowhere to be seen now. Likely he'd already gone to the chapel to do some last-minute preparations before the ceremony.

Her sister Anna stepped up next to her, linking her arm with Mirabelle's. "Isn't this exciting? A wedding!"

Mirabelle gave her younger sister's hand a pat, Anna's blonde hair shining in the sun. It was exciting. "Our brothers don't look all that thrilled."

Anna giggled. "Why do men think it's their job to be grumpy about everything? What could be more exciting than finding love?"

Mirabelle's mouth twitched with an answer that she didn't speak. She wasn't all that interested in marriage either.

Someday she would marry. But first, she fully intended to become a jewel of the ton. Of course, she still wasn't exactly certain how to make her dream come true.

She hadn't grown up among the very people she wished to impress. Would they sense it?

"What took you so long?" Fulton grunted, cracking his knuckles as she and Anna approached.

Neither of them were the least bit put out by his tone, his look of irritation, or his ominous cracking. They knew better. All of their brothers were intent upon their sisters' well being.

Their father had split his time between his legitimate family and them. It had meant that her brothers were often called upon for their care the women of the family and it was a role they filled without complaint.

And whatever their flaws, they took their job seriously.

A fact that Mirabelle had always appreciated. But looking at them now, she knew none of them could escort her about London this fall when she'd attend several events to prepare for her debut this winter.

Ace and Emily would help, of course.

But she needed more...

She needed a man who understood what other lords looked for in a lady.

Her gaze fluttered down the line of carriages where another group of guests stood.

First, there was the Duke of Upton. The man's stern features and broad chest managed to be even more intimidating than any of her brothers'. She shivered as she dismissed the idea. She'd never gain the help of a man like that.

And then there was the Earl of Somersworth. His blond hair and charming features did make him appear as though he were out of a fairy tale.

Could she ever convince a man like that to help her? A frown knit her brow as she considered. Likely not.

Finally, her gaze landed on the third man in the bunch, Baron Boxby.

Emily's brother. His brown hair glinted in the sun, picking up the few blonde streaks that colored the strands.

She knew his eyes were a warm brown, and though he was just as masculine as the others, there was something kinder that colored his eyes. Just like Emily's.

He was the one that could help her. She was sure of it.

But she also knew that she couldn't come right out and ask. It wasn't done, and besides, why would he even want to?

But she was not a proper lady, after all, and she'd grown up on the east side. She knew all sorts of tricks that a woman born and bred of money would never think to employ and she had the perfect plan, to gain his aid...

He'd never even know what hit him.

———

Kenneth Boxby, baron of the same name, stood with his two best friends and drew in a breath of the crisp morning air.

Today, his sister would wed. With their parents deceased for the past decade, he'd taken on her guardianship with all the vigor an eighteen-year-old might apply to the task. And now, at the age of eight and twenty, he was free.

Not that he didn't love his sister. He did. More than anything in this world. And he would have been her guardian for the next ten years. Honestly, he'd have cared for her for all of his life.

But now, on the precipice of her wedding, he realized he was free.

His other friends, The Duke of Upton on his right, large and craggy, and Earl of Somersworth on his left, the definition of handsome, had had years of debaucherous fun.

Sure, he joined them to box, to attend dinners at their gentlemen's club, and he even went out for the occasional night of gaming.

But where his friends might stumble home in the wee hours of the morning, he always returned home long before that.

He had Emily to escort, or to provide company, or to aid with lessons.

But that was all in the past. Now he was free to stay out all hours, to indulge as much and whenever he chose, and he was eager to take full advantage.

Ken shifted even as Upton looked across the twenty yards that separated them from Ace's family. "That sister of theirs sure is a something," he muttered in his usual fashion of saying something that actually gave very little away.

Kenneth felt himself stiffen as he followed Upton's gaze. Mirabelle.

His sister's best friend and a constant source of irritation for himself, though he couldn't quite explain why. She was beyond pretty, a delicate sort of beauty with dark brown and large brown eyes that always seemed to shine. Her nose was pert with just the tiniest upturn, her lips full and wide, often with a smile playing at their corners.

She was slender and small, in stark contrast to her hulking brothers, not that she didn't have her share of curves. But was small enough to almost be fragile.

And whenever their eyes met, she unsettled him.

He was a man approaching his thirties. He understood lust. The raw heat of it, the want, the need.

But when he looked at Mirabelle, the feeling that coursed through him was different. Less raw and more complicated.

So he mostly ignored her.

But the idea of Upton laying favor on her made something rip in his chest. He turned to his friend, a dark emotion curling his lip. "Ace is now my family. And our business partner. Stay away from his sisters."

Upton's eyes widened with surprise. Which in and of itself was shocking. Upton never looked unprepared. Derisive, often. Bored, even more so.

"Calm yourself, Boxby," Upton rumbled, narrowing his gaze. "She's far too young and too fair for my liking. It's only odd because she's the only blonde in the entire family. Makes me wonder if she is their full sibling."

Belatedly, Ken realized Upton hadn't been talking about Mirabelle at all. He'd been discussing Anna. What was wrong with him?

"Both of Ace's sisters are beauties," Somersworth murmured, as much to himself as them. "and considering Ace stole Emily right out from under me, I wonder if I ought—"

But even as the simmering tension swelled inside him again, Upton cut their friend off. "You just heard Boxby. He says they are off limits."

Ken's jaw tightened. The truth was so much more complicated. Not even he understood it, so he said nothing as they climbed into one of the waiting carriages.

The three of them settle into the seats, Upton, seemingly determined to steer the subject to safer waters. "So… the club…"

The club. Hell's Corner. And Ken's first act of real male independence. He'd bought a share in a gaming hell along with Upton and Somersworth and all the other Smith brothers. The irritable lot of them.

"The club," Somersworth repeated, raking a hand through his hair. "It's opening next week. Yes?"

"Yes," Ken answered, shifting in his seat. They'd shut the doors two months prior to redecorate the inside, restock, and hire new staff. The club was being transformed to look far more like the Den of Sins, their brother club, which was also under repair after a fire had charred the inside two months prior.

"And when will we return to London?" Upton asked, shifting

forward. The duke always became restless in the country. It was too quiet, too serene.

"In a few days," Ken answered. "Though you don't have to wait with me. I'll travel back with the Smiths regardless, and see Emily settled."

"Always the dutiful brother," Somersworth replied as the carriage stopped outside the chapel.

They emerged from the vehicle just as the Smiths were unloading from the two more carriages, and he caught sight of Mirabelle as her brother Rush handed her out.

Without thought, he crossed the short distance to the Smiths, stopping just a few feet from Mirabelle as Rush reached into the vehicle once again to aid Anna.

"Good morning," Mirabelle said, giving him that sweet smile. The one that made him both hot and cold. "What a beautiful day for a wedding."

"Don't be ridiculous, Mira," Rush called over his shoulder. "Men don't care about the weather for weddings."

Tris joined them, coming from yet another carriage as he swept a hand through his overlong hair. "I'd go even further and say that men would prefer pouring rain. Suits the mood of the event."

Mirabelle clucked her tongue, giving Tris a disapproving glare. "Don't be absurd. Weddings are joyful events."

Tris gave his sister a dark frown in return, but she didn't seem the least bit bothered. "I suppose I can make an exception for Ace. This wedding has brought a great deal to our family, and your sister seems like a nice enough lady." Tris's gaze flicked to Ken. "I meant no offense, Lord Boxby."

Ken gave a quick jerk of his chin. "I didn't take any." Truth be told, he wasn't eager to wed himself.

Tris gave an answering bow, holding his arm out to Mirabelle. But she only gave him that smile of hers... the one that looked stunning but hinted at something under the surface. "Lord Boxby will escort me."

His brows rose. He would. But why did asked him? He had to

confess that his curiosity had been peeked, as he stepped next to her and offered his arm.

As her hand slipped into his elbow, fingers small and feminine as the one word he'd been hunting for suddenly popped to the forefront of his thoughts.

Mirabelle Smith was a delightful mystery. One a man wished to solve.

A Bet with a Baron is the first books in the Lords of Temptation series!! A Bet with a Baron will be for sale on major retailers!!!

Keep up with all the latest news, sales, freebies, and releases by joining my newsletter!

www.tammyandresen.com

Hugs!

OTHER TITLES BY TAMMY

The Dark Duke's Legacy

Her Wicked White

Her Wanton White

His Wallflower White

Her Willful White

Her Wanton White

His White Wager

Her White Wedding

Lords of Scandal

Duke of Daring

Marquess of Malice

Earl of Exile

Viscount of Vice

Baron of Bad

Earl of Sin

Earl of Gold

Earl of Baxter

Duke of Decandence

Marquess of Menace

Duke of Dishonor

Baron of Blasphemy

Viscount of Vanity

Earl of Infamy

Laird of Longing

Fairfield Fairy Tales

Stealing a Lady's Heart

Hunting for a Lady's Heart

Entrapping a Lord's Love: Coming in February of 2018

American Historical Romance

Lily in Bloom

Midnight Magic

The Golden Rules of Love

Boxsets!!

Taming the Duke's Heart Books 1-3

American Brides

A Laird to Love

Wicked Lords of London

ABOUT THE AUTHOR

Tammy Andresen lives with her husband and three children just outside of Boston, Massachusetts. She grew up on the Seacoast of Maine, where she spent countless days dreaming up stories in blueberry fields and among the scrub pines that line the coast. Her mother loved to spin a yarn and Tammy filled many hours listening to her mother retell the classics. It was inevitable that at the age of eighteen, she headed off to Simmons College, where she studied English literature and education. She never left Massachusetts but some of her heart still resides in Maine and her family visits often.

Find out more about Tammy:
http://www.tammyandresen.com/
https://www.facebook.com/authortammyandresen
https://twitter.com/TammyAndresen
https://www.pinterest.com/tammy_andresen/
https://plus.google.com/+TammyAndresen/

Printed in Great Britain
by Amazon

22332100R00079